Meet ✏ *f!*

Chelsea—A brainy **Alicia Silverstone** type with a southern twang, she's shocked by the tell-all topics of *Trash*. But by summer's end, *Trash* could be telling Chelsea's big secret!

Karma—This Asian beauty is a downtown Manhattan diva with **Fran Drescher**'s voice. Late nights? Cool clubs? Great shopping? Money to be made? Call Karma!

Lisha—Oh-so-cool, hotter than **Demi Moore**, they call her "Luscious Lisha" on the *Trash* set. She's not the same fat, awkward girl that Chelsea grew up with . . . is she?

Sky—Sweet, laid back, a T-shirt and jeans kind of guy who's a whiz with a movie camera, he gets mistaken a lot on the street for **Keanu Reeves** and is everyone's best bud.

Alan—This sensitive writer from Texas is sure the trash on *Trash* will give him tons of material. If **Johnny Depp** were a writer, he'd be Alan!

Nick—A Canadian slacker with a heart of gold. Chelsea's madly in love with this **Brad Pitt** double, but she has to wait in line behind their famous boss, Jazz Stewart!

continued . . .

the bosses

Jazz—The gorgeous **Darryl Hannah**–ish host of *Trash* is afraid of nothing, whether it's posing for nude pix on the beach in France, riding her Harley onto the set while clad in a bikini, or having three boyfriends at once. Because it's all *Trash,* isn't it?

Roxanne—The beautiful, icy, and ambitious associate producer, she's **Sharon Stone** at age twenty-something and loathes all interns on principle! Behind her back, they call her "Bigfoot" . . . after those gigantic size-twelve dawgs!

Barry—The slick producer with the power, he's willing to help Chelsea go big places at *Trash.* The question is, is she willing to pay his price?

Sumtimes—Can a girl have a shaved head and still be gorgeous? Yes! The interns' fave producer got her nickname because she sometimes calls herself Cindy, sometimes Julia, sometimes *whatever*!

TRASH:
it's not just a job,
it's an adventure!

TRASH

truth or scare

Cherie Bennett

and

Jeff Gottesfeld

BERKLEY BOOKS, NEW YORK

TRASH: TRUTH OR SCARE

A Berkley Book / published by arrangement with
the authors

PRINTING HISTORY
Berkley edition / February 1998

The Putnam Berkley World Wide Web site address is
http://www.berkley.com

ISBN: 0-425-16188-9

BERKLEY®
Berkley Books are published by The Berkley Publishing Group,
a member of Penguin Putnam Inc.,
200 Madison Avenue,
New York, New York 10016.
BERKLEY and the "B" design
are trademarks belonging to Berkley Publishing Corporation.

PRINTED IN THE UNITED STATES OF AMERICA

10 9 8 7 6 5 4 3 2 1

*To the first all-teen
cast and crew of* Cyra & Rocky:
*Harrison Gray, Claire Jarman, Zoë Jarman,
Meredith Jones, Josh Rew, and Freya Sachs.*

You guys rock!

truth or scare

"I can't stand this," Lisha Bishop announced, looking around the living room of their apartment. "It's too empty without Karma." She sat heavily in the overstuffed armchair, leaned her head back, and closed her eyes. They felt dry and gritty from lack of sleep.

Chelsea Jennings, one of Lisha's two roommates, plopped down on the couch. "I was so scared—"

"I'm *still* scared," Lisha said. Her eyes popped open. "Do you think Karma could still—"

"She's going to live," Chelsea said firmly. "Dr. Tucci said she was going to pull through."

"Yeah, well, what if he's wrong?" Lisha asked. "I don't have a lot of faith in doctors."

"Doctors just saved Karma's life," Chelsea pointed out softly.

Lisha didn't answer. She looked out the dirt-streaked window and realized that the sun had come up and she hadn't even noticed. Then she leaned her head against the back of the chair and closed her eyes again. She and Chelsea had just returned from spending ten hours at the hospital, where their best friend and third roommate, Karma Kushner, had almost died.

And to think Karma almost died because she was doing a good deed for her twin sister, Janelle, who seems to hate Karma's guts, Lisha thought. *Tell me there is any justice in the world.*

Lisha thought back to the time, earlier in the summer, when Karma had found out that she actually had a twin sister. Born in Korea, both had been adopted as babies, and neither had known of the other's existence. Once Karma found out, she wanted to become friends with Janelle, but preppie, standoffish Janelle seemed to want to pretend that Karma didn't exist.

Until she needed emergency surgery and wanted one of Karma's kidneys, that is, Lisha recalled. *And Karma had a bad reaction to the anesthetic and almost died.*

There was a knock on the door. Lisha opened her eyes. "It's either a very polite psycho-killer or one of the guys," she decided.

"The guys" she was referring to were Nick Shaw, Sky Addison, and Alan Van Kleef, who lived directly across the hall from them. All six of them were summer interns at the world's trashiest and most popular TV teen talk show, *Trash.*

"Please watch the 'psycho-killer' jokes," Chelsea said as she padded to the door.

"Oops," Lisha said, blowing her shaggy bangs out of her eyes. "I keep forgetting."

As incredible as it seemed, Chelsea's father had actually been a very famous mass murderer, who gunned down more than twenty people in a Burger Barn restaurant when Chelsea was a baby. Chelsea's mom had changed their name and hidden their identity, and Chelsea had lived in fear for all these years that someone would find out the truth. Well, someone had. And that someone was Jazz, the gorgeous host of *Trash,* who had outted Chelsea's horrible secret on national TV.

"Hi," Chelsea said as she opened the door to Alan, who was carrying some kind of casserole dish. The smell wafted through the apartment.

"Whatever that is, it smells great," Lisha said, sniffing appreciatively.

"My mom's recipe for killer macaroni-and-cheese casserole," Alan said. "I made this huge thing of it last week and froze it, and I nuked some for y'all. I figured you'd be hungry. I know it's kind of a weird breakfast, but it's been a weird night."

Lisha smiled at Alan. *He's so sweet,* she thought as she watched him carry the casserole into their little kitchen, off the living room. *I could never find a better guy than him. He's also smart, and funny, and sensitive, and he wants to be a writer. And he looks just like*

3

Johnny Depp. So what more could I possibly want?

Sparks, Lisha thought, mentally answering her own question. *Like the kind of sparks I have with Sky.*

"You are a lifesaver," Chelsea declared. "I'm starving."

"God, there are a zillion fat grams in that," Lisha said, groaning.

"Lisha, you don't have to worry about fat grams," Alan said, as he opened their cupboard and took out some bowls for them.

"Ha, you didn't know me when I was a porker." Lisha pushed herself out of the chair and went to sniff the casserole up close. "I'm gaining weight just by breathing macaroni-and-cheese *air*."

Alan filled a dish and handed it to her. "I would love you fat or thin," he said lightly.

"So would I," Sky said, walking into the apartment. "Hey, didn't anyone ever tell you guys it's dangerous to leave your front door open?"

Lisha tried not to notice how cute Sky looked. He had on jeans and a denim shirt, which was unbuttoned. His hair was sexily mussed. The muscles on his tan stomach rippled.

"Yeah, people like you might just walk in," Lisha quipped.

"She only says things like that because she's crazy about me," Sky told Chelsea. He leaned

4

against the wall and folded his arms. "So, do we all call in sick to *Trash*? It's after eight o'clock now."

"Nick doesn't have to call," Chelsea said, popping some of the casserole into her mouth. "Jazz will forgive him for anything."

"Try to remember that the two of you made up," Alan reminded her.

"I know," Chelsea said. "But that doesn't mean Jazz isn't still after him."

"We can't all call in sick," Alan said. "Bigfoot would kill us."

Bigfoot, so nicknamed because of the size of her feet, also known as Roxanne Renault, was one of their bosses at *Trash*. She looked like a young redheaded version of Sharon Stone.

And she was perhaps the nastiest person any of them had ever met.

"Bigfoot can eat dirt and die," Lisha said, savoring a bite of the casserole. "None of us have had any sleep!"

"You think she cares?" Alan asked.

"Doubtful," Chelsea admitted. "But maybe if we call Sumtimes—"

Sumtimes was another one of the producers at *Trash*. Her last name was Sumtimes, but she changed her first name every week or so, so everyone simply referred to her by her last name.

"Good idea," Lisha said. She picked up the cordless phone and quickly punched in Sumtimes's direct number. "I know Sumtimes

5

works hard, but even she won't be in at eight o'clock. I'll leave a message on her—"

"Sumtimes," the producer barked into the phone.

"Oh, hi," Lisha said, taken aback to hear the producer's voice. "I thought I'd get your voice mail. It's Lisha."

"What's up?" Sumtimes said briskly.

Lisha quickly filled her in on Karma's emergency surgery, and how all the *Trash* interns had just now returned home after spending the night at the hospital.

"Wow," Sumtimes breathed. "So is Karma okay?"

"Yeah, we think so," Lisha said.

"Give me the name of the hospital," Sumtimes said. "I'm sure Jazz will want to send flowers."

Lisha gave her the information. "So listen, we're all totally fried. None of us have had any sleep. So we're going to crash—"

"Bad idea," Sumtimes interrupted.

"But—"

"Jazz doesn't think lack of sleep is a reason to miss work," Sumtimes said. "The only one who has an excuse not to come in is Karma. Maybe."

"Gee, that's big of her," Lisha said dryly.

"I'll tell you what," Sumtimes said. "You guys sleep for a few hours, and get in at noon, okay? I'll cover for you."

"You're a peach," Lisha said. She hung up

and relayed the conversation to Chelsea and Alan.

"I'm already in bed," Chelsea said, slipping out of her clogs. She kissed Alan on the cheek. "Thanks for the food."

"I'll tell Nick the good news," Alan offered. He looked over at Lisha. "Need a wake-up call?"

"Nah, I'm cool," Lisha said.

"Okay." Alan nodded. "I'll leave the food—y'all can eat it later." He gave Lisha a boyish grin and left.

"I could come in and tell you a bedtime story," Sky offered, giving Lisha a sexy half smile.

"Wow, how could I possibly turn that down?" Lisha asked sarcastically.

Sky sighed dramatically. "When it comes to you, Lish, I am charm-free." He yawned as he walked to the door. "Man, I'm beat. So, I'll see you guys later."

"Now, that is a great guy," Chelsea said. She lifted her T-shirt over her head.

"Sky is too full of himself," Lisha commented.

"I didn't mean Sky," Chelsea said. "I meant Alan."

"So, why aren't you going out with him, then?" Lisha asked pointedly. She dropped her empty bowl in the sink.

Chelsea gave her a look. "Remember a little someone named Nick? Besides, Alan is yours."

"He's not mine," Lisha said grumpily.

"But you two are—"

"I don't know what we are," Lisha snapped. She sighed. "Oh, ignore me. I'm suffering from sleep deficit and fat-gram overload." She began to unbutton her cropped, black jersey shirt and headed down the hall with Chelsea. "After work, we'll head back to the hospital, right?"

"Right," Chelsea agreed. She stopped just outside the door of her room. "Karma was incredibly brave, wasn't she?"

"Incredibly something," Lisha said, with her patented Lisha shrug. "Dumb, maybe."

"How can you say that?"

"All I know is that if I found out I had a twin sister who dissed me as bad as Janelle disses Karma, I'd think three or four times before I risked my life for her."

Chelsea cocked her head at Lisha. "You're not nearly as tough as you pretend to be."

"How do you know?" Lisha asked.

Chelsea smiled. "Because I've known you for too long. Underneath that tough-girl thing, you are a big softie."

"I don't know, Chels," Lisha said, her voice low. "I'm not so sure anymore."

Chelsea studied her friend. "Because of what happened with Harley?"

"Hey, I'm way too tired to get all heavy right now," Lisha said, trying to keep her voice light. "We'll talk later. Okay?"

"Okay," Chelsea agreed.

Lisha pulled off her clothes and dropped them in a pile, quickly set the little alarm clock on her nightstand, and climbed into her water bed. But as exhausted as she was, she couldn't sleep. Images kept zapping through her mind, like quick, disjointed scenes from a movie.

She thought back to what would have been her senior year in high school, but because she had graduated early, her parents had treated her to a trip to Europe. That was where she had met Harley, her first, her only, really serious boyfriend.

God, I was so young and so stupid, she recalled. *I never thought a guy as cute as Harley would fall for fat, hick, little me. I thought he was helping me when he got me hooked on diet pills. I thought it was a miracle when I lost all that weight. And everyone started telling me how cute I looked, like a young version of Demi Moore. I ate that up. I never knew Harley was a drug dealer, or a drug addict.*

Maybe I just didn't want to know.

And then when he showed up here in New York, and he had that gun—

No. She wouldn't let herself think about all that now. It had been too horrible. She willed herself to put it out of her mind.

But as horrible as those recollections were, the next images that came into Lisha's mind were happy. Such as the day she'd found out that out of thousands of applicants, she had actually been chosen as a summer intern by *Trash*. Or that when she'd shown up at the apartment in New York that *Trash* had rented for the three female interns, she'd found out that one of the other interns was none other than her very best friend from childhood, Chelsea Jennings.

Chelsea had grown up to be loyal, smart, down-to-earth, and a great friend. She'd also grown up to look like Alicia Silverstone, and the combination of her all-American looks and great personality made her very popular with guys.

Lisha smiled as she thought about how close she had grown to Chelsea again, and how much she loved Karma, too.

Karma was truly one of a kind. Raised by Jewish former-hippie parents who owned a health-food-and-book store on Long Island, she considered herself a Korean Jewish-American princess. She was incredibly smart, and she played the stock market. She lived on junk food, had more energy than any six other people Lisha knew, and created her own fashions that combined designer pieces with cheap chic. She was also hilariously funny, and sounded just like Fran Drescher on *The Nanny*.

They are the two best friends I've ever had in my life, Lisha realized. *I'd do anything for them.* She turned over in bed and tried to find a comfortable position. Her throat felt a little sore.

I hope it's just exhaustion, she thought. *Because I sure don't have time to get sick.*

She snuggled her head into her pillow and

tried to will herself to fall asleep. Alan's face swam before her eyes. And then Sky's.

It was maddening.

I wonder why it's so much easier to get close to a girlfriend than it is to get close to a guy, she mused.

Because guys lie to you and hurt you and break your heart, came the answer in her head.

"Not Alan," she said out loud. "Alan is nothing like Harley."

It was true. Lisha really believed that Alan would never hurt her. And she liked him so much.

But why, then, were all of her dreams filled with images of being in Sky's arms, Sky's lips on hers?

Alan felt safe. Sky felt dangerous.

I actually believe that if I got fat again—God forbid—Alan would love me anyway, Lisha thought. *But not Sky. Never. No matter what he says.*

So, how do I choose? Lisha wondered. *How does any girl choose between friendship and passion?*

And how many people do you hurt if you make the wrong choice, like I did with Harley?

With that troubling thought in mind, she finally drifted off to sleep.

Her dream seemed so real. She was in Sky's arms. He was kissing her, his body pressed to hers. She felt dizzy with happiness, passion, she never wanted the moment to end—

The shrill ring of the telephone next to her bed snapped her awake.

Groggily, she reached for it, just as Chelsea picked up in her room.

"Hello?" they both said at the same time.

"Lisha, Chelsea, it's Wendy," a nervous voice said into the phone.

Lisha woke up immediately. Wendy was Karma's mom.

"Is Karma . . . ?" Lisha began.

"She's had another complication," Wendy said, her voice choked with emotion. "It's serious."

"Oh, God, Wendy, I'm so sorry," Chelsea breathed.

"Please, can you come back to the hospital?" Wendy asked. "Karma asked for you, and then . . . then something happened and they made me leave her room, and the doctors and nurses ran in—"

"We're on our way," Lisha said. She hung up the phone and scrambled into her clothes.

She met a wild-eyed Chelsea at the front door.

Wordlessly, they walked out, locking the door behind them.

"She's going to be fine," Lisha said as they traveled down in the ancient elevator, which had, for once, mercifully been waiting on their floor.

"I know," Chelsea said.

"She *has* to be fine," Lisha said, her voice breaking.

Chelsea took Lisha's hand.

There was nothing more to say.

And all Lisha could think was that, suddenly, her love life didn't seem all that important at all.

"Demetrius?" Lisha asked.

Karma's boyfriend, who was slumped over in a chair in the waiting room of the hospital, looked up as Lisha and Chelsea hurried toward him. His long, muscular body barely fit in the small, molded chair. His flowing hair, usually so perfectly groomed, was tied back in a messy ponytail. His red-rimmed eyes told a scary story.

"How is she?" Chelsea asked, her voice fearful.

"She's stable but critical," Demetrius said, his voice low and hoarse.

Lisha coughed, her throat feeling scratchier than ever. "What happened?" she asked, sitting down next to him.

Demetrius ran his hand across the stubble that had grown on his chin. He'd been there all night. "The doctors aren't really sure. Her blood pressure just plummeted. They thought they were going to lose her—"

"Oh, God," Chelsea whispered, clapping her hand to her mouth.

"She's in intensive care," Demetrius said. He shook his head. "I just . . . I can't believe this is happening!"

"Where are Karma's parents?" Lisha asked.

"In the ICU with her," Demetrius answered. "They only let them go in for a few minutes at a time, so they'll be out soon—oh, there they are, now."

Wendy and Marty Kushner hurried over to Lisha and Chelsea and hugged both girls tight.

"Thank you for coming," Wendy said, pressing a Kleenex to her eyes.

"Don't thank us," Lisha said. "We love Karma. Can we get you anything? Coffee? Some food?" She began to cough again.

"Are you sick?" Wendy asked Lisha, concerned.

"It's nothing." Lisha waved her hand dismissively, though the truth was she was beginning to feel achy and feverish. "So, what can we do for you?"

"You're here," Wendy said. "That's a lot." She sat heavily in one of the ugly orange plastic chairs.

"I just . . . how could this be happening?" Marty asked. "I feel like it's my fault. I'm the one who talked her into—"

"She made her own choice," Lisha insisted firmly.

"She didn't want to disappoint us," Wendy protested tearfully.

Demetrius reached over for Wendy's hand. "I believe that Karma is going to be fine. I do."

"I do, too," Chelsea said. "I promised that we'd throw her a party when she gets out of here, and I'm planning it already."

"It's going to be a major blowout," Lisha agreed, coughing again. She shivered a little, and sweat broke out on her forehead. "With all of Karma's favorite junk food."

Wendy managed to smile wearily at her daughter's friends. "She'd like that."

"How is Janelle doing?" Chelsea asked.

"Who cares how Janelle is doing?" Lisha asked sharply. "If it wasn't for Janelle, Karma wouldn't be here!"

"It's not Janelle's fault," Marty said. "Her parents are with her now. She's fine."

"Figures," Lisha muttered to herself. She coughed again.

"Are you sure you're not getting sick?" Chelsea asked her.

"I'm fine," Lisha insisted.

"Mr. and Mrs. Kushner?"

They all looked up to see Dr. Tucci walking toward them.

Wendy and Marty stood up, white-faced.

"I just wanted to let you know. Karma's blood pressure has stabilized. She's awake."

Wendy's face lit up. "She's . . . ?"

Dr. Tucci nodded. "If everything goes well,

17

we'll be able to move her out of the ICU this afternoon."

"Thank God," Marty murmured. He shook Dr. Tucci's hand. "And thank you. I know you've been here all night—"

"It's my job," Dr. Tucci said simply. He smiled. "Your daughter gave me two messages for you all just now."

"What's that?" Wendy asked.

"Let's see, she wanted you to know she is still CEO of the Kushner Agency, and she wanted to know how soon she can get a cup of coffee."

Everyone in the waiting room laughed with relief. Karma had pretended to be Chelsea's agent, and had negotiated a huge tell-all book deal for her that would have required Chelsea to spill everything about what it was like to be the daughter of a mass murderer.

And Karma was hooked on black coffee.

"Can I see her?" Demetrius asked eagerly.

"No, not yet," Dr. Tucci said. "But soon. I promise."

"Thank you again, doctor," Marty said, shaking the doctor's hand.

"My pleasure." Dr. Tucci smiled, then turned and walked away.

Wendy sank into the nearest chair. "This has been the longest night of my life." Her husband took her into his arms.

"Look at that," Chelsea whispered to Lisha. "They love each other so much."

"Sweet," Lisha replied. She coughed again and another shiver ran through her.

Chelsea put her hand on her friend's forehead. "Hey, you have a fever!"

"I don't—"

Demetrius walked over and felt Lisha's forehead, too. "Yep. Fever. The last place you belong is a hospital."

"That doesn't make much sense," Lisha replied weakly. She was feeling worse by the minute.

"Yeah, it does," Demetrius said. "You could infect a lot of people with compromised immune systems here. You need to get home."

"I'll take her," Chelsea offered. "And then I'll come back—"

"No, you need to get some rest," Wendy told Chelsea.

"But—"

"Please." Wendy put her hand on Chelsea's shoulder. "There's no point in all of you getting sick. I'll call you as soon as Karma can have visitors."

"Okay," Chelsea said reluctantly. She hugged Karma's mom again. "If you need anything at all—"

"I know," Wendy said, smiling. "Now, take Lisha home and get her into bed."

"Dr. Sky reporting for duty," Sky said, carrying a tray filled with soup and juice into Lisha's room.

It was that evening, and Lisha had been sleeping all afternoon. Her throat felt raw, her nose was stuffed up, and she felt achy all over.

Oh, great, she thought as she ran her hand through her messy hair. *Why does he have to see me looking like this? Of course, the funny thing is, it wouldn't bother me to have Alan see me like this.*

"It's not homemade soup—I opened a can of chicken noodle and nuked it, but, hey, it's the thought that counts." Sky set the tray on Lisha's nightstand.

"Why are you being so nice?" she asked.

"Because I *am* nice," Sky replied, sitting on the edge of her bed.

"No, Alan is nice," Lisha corrected. "You want to get into my pants."

Sky put his hand over his heart. "I am injured."

"You just can't take the truth," Lisha said. She reached for the bowl of soup.

"Yes, I can," Sky protested. "What, I'm supposed to deny being attracted to you? Not that you look so delicious right now, by the way—"

"I'm sick," Lisha snapped. "I look sick."

"I don't know," Sky said, with a dramatic sigh. "On TV, beautiful girls still look beautiful when they're sick. This is a major disappointment to me."

"Cope." Lisha blew on a spoonful of soup and took a sip.

"Sick and testy," Sky said lightly. "See if I

work my fingers to the bone opening any more soup cans for you."

"I'm sorry," Lisha said. "I'm a terrible patient. Thanks for the soup." She took another sip. "How's Karma?"

"Out of the ICU," Sky reported. "Her condition has been upgraded. She's begging for a bagel with cream cheese."

Lisha smiled. "That's my Karma." She coughed deeply.

Sky frowned. "Maybe you should see a doctor."

"It's just a cold."

"How do you know?" a voice from the doorway asked. Lisha looked up. It was Alan. He was carrying a bouquet of flowers and a carton of ice cream.

"Hi," Lisha said. "Are those for me?"

"They sure aren't for him." Alan cocked his head at Sky. "What are you doing here?"

"Visiting the sick and needy," Sky said, getting up from Lisha's bed. He gave Alan a hard look.

"I can take care of her," Alan said.

"So can I," Sky replied.

Are they actually fighting over me? Lisha wondered. *I don't want that. Alan and Sky are best friends!*

"Look, I don't need anyone to take care of me, okay?" she told them, coughing again.

"Oh yeah, right," Alan agreed sarcastically. He walked over to Lisha and kissed her on the forehead. "Temp is down, I see." He handed her the ice cream. "Got a vase?" He looked around the room.

"There's a glass you can use in the bathroom," Lisha said, then smacked her forehead. "God, I just realized! I never called into work before I fell asleep—"

"Chelsea called in for you," Alan said as he went into the bathroom. He came out with the flowers arranged in a glass of water, which he set on her nightstand.

"How was work?" Lisha asked them, opening the ice cream.

"It was *Trash*," Sky said with a shrug.

"The news of the day is that Jazz says she's finally naming the father of her baby on the air on Friday."

Lisha paused while spooning some ice cream into her mouth. "Nick?"

"Not according to Nick," Alan said.

"God, Chelsea would just die." Lisha sighed, shaking her head. She ate another bite of ice cream. "I heard that calories don't count when you're sick."

"You heard right," Alan said, giving her a boyish grin. "Eat to your heart's content."

Just then Chelsea appeared in the doorway. "Hey Alan, Nick just banged on the door. There's a phone call for you."

"Thanks," Alan said. "Be right back."

Chelsea smiled at Lisha. "Feel any better?"

"Ice cream works wonders for me," Lisha said.

"Need anything?" Chelsea asked.

"You must be beat," Lisha realized. "Did you get any sleep at all before you went to work?"

Chelsea shook her head no. "And now I'm buzzing on too much caffeine."

"Well, go lie down so you don't get sick, too," Lisha instructed her.

Sky sat back down on the bed. "How about an alcohol rub?"

"How about not?"

"What, you think I'm just trying to get you naked?"

"Probably." Lisha coughed again and shivered. "I think I need more aspirin."

Sky got Lisha the aspirin from the bathroom and handed it to her. She swallowed it down with a mouthful of ice cream.

"I guess I should let you rest," Sky said. He sat back on the edge of her bed. Slowly, he reached his hand out and stroked the damp hair off her cheek. A shiver ran through Lisha, but this time it wasn't from her fever.

How can I react that way just because he touched me? she thought.

"Will you call me if you need anything?" Sky asked, his voice low.

"Probably not," Lisha said, keeping her voice light. "I'll call Chelsea."

"You know you make me crazy—"

Lisha shrugged.

Sky leaned closer to her. She could see the sexy outline of his lips. She moved her face away from him. "My breath must be all yucky—"

"Not," Sky said.

"Well, I don't want to give you any germs," she said quickly.

"I don't care," Sky responded.

"I'm going out with Alan!" Lisha reminded him sharply.

Sky pulled away. "That's right."

"Right."

"I forgot."

"No, you didn't."

"You're right." Sky got up from the bed. "Just please ask yourself why you're going out with him, Lish."

"I know why. Because he's a great guy and I really like him," she said firmly.

"He *is* a great guy," Sky agreed. His eyes searched hers. "But that isn't the answer to my question."

"Yeah, it is."

Sky just stared at her.

"It *is*!" she insisted.

"You and I are going to happen," Sky stated calmly. "Eventually."

"You have the biggest ego—"

"No," Sky said. "But I'm not blind. And I'm not stupid. You're running scared, Lish. I just wish you'd run in my direction." He walked to the door, then turned back to her. "I have a feeling we're having the same dreams at night. And neither one of those dreams stars Alan."

Lisha watched Sky walk out the door. She lay down on her pillow and pulled the blankets up to her chin. Sky was right. She had been dreaming about him. And her dreams were so hot they were embarrassing.

But Alan wrote her poetry. He took care of her.

The phone next to the bed rang. She picked it up.

"Hello?"

"You let them keep me here without junk food?" came a weak, nasal, New York–accented voice.

"Karma!" Lisha exclaimed, sitting up.

"They won't let me have coffee, either. You've got to get me out of here."

"I'm so glad to hear your voice!" Lisha said fervently.

"Yeah, me, too," Karma said. "Wow, what an experience."

"How are you feeling?"

"Like I just lost a kidney—ha-ha," Karma said. "My mother wants to talk to you."

"Lisha?" Wendy's voice came through the phone.

"I'm here," Lisha said. "Is she better?"

"Much," Wendy said happily. "Dr. Tucci says if everything goes well, she can come home in a few days."

"I'm so glad." The relief was evident in her voice.

"I just wanted to thank you girls again," Wendy said. "You and Chelsea are beautiful old souls."

Lisha laughed, which made her cough. "That's a little too New Age huggie-veggie for me."

Wendy laughed, too. "I'll bring you guys a true feast from our health-food store to celebrate sometime soon."

"No tofu for me," Lisha declared.

"Karma wants to say one more thing," Wendy said. "But that's it, honey," Lisha could hear her telling Karma. "You have to rest."

"Lish?" Karma asked.

"What?"

"If you love me, you'll bring me a Hershey's bar tomorrow. Jumbo-sized."

"We'll bring you a truckload of them," Lisha promised, then she said good-bye and hung up.

Chelsea padded into her room. "Who called? I was in the bathroom."

"Karma!" Lisha told her with a smile. "Isn't that great?"

"Fantastic," Chelsea cried.

"She wants junk food."

"Now I *know* she's okay," Chelsea said, grinning.

Lisha drew her knees up to her chin. "Did you see how great Demetrius was? He really loves her."

"Yeah."

"It must be great, to be loved like that by a guy who is that hot."

"Alan loves you like that," Chelsea reminded her.

Lisha cocked her head at Chelsea. "He used to love you."

"No—"

"He did," Lisha insisted. "Sometimes I think he still does."

Chelsea looked thoughtful. "I just think Alan is a really, really caring guy. And he wants to be loved. So . . . do you love him?"

"I don't know," Lisha admitted. "I don't even think I know what love is." She pushed her bangs out of her eyes. "Do you love Nick?"

Chelsea leaned against the door frame. "Yeah."

"Even if he and Jazz—"

"But they didn't sleep together," Chelsea said. "That's what Nick said. And I believe him."

"You didn't believe him for a long time," Lisha reminded her, coughing again.

"Well, I was wrong. You told me so yourself. If you love someone, you have to trust them."

Lisha nodded. "I think I'm going back to sleep. Could you put the ice cream in the fridge for me?"

"Sure," Chelsea said, getting the ice cream from the nightstand. "Sleep tight."

Lisha snuggled down into bed. She thought

about what Chelsea had just said to her: *If you love someone, you have to trust them.*

She knew she could trust Alan.

But knowing how Sky could get under her skin made her feel too vulnerable. So how, how could she ever trust her heart to Sky?

Lisha adjusted her earphones and pressed the button to start the next tape. She, Chelsea, Alan, and Nick were in the room they referred to as Sicko-Central. Their job was to transcribe the tapes from the 900-I'M-TRASH phone line. Many of the people who called actually believed they would be talking directly to Jazz. It was really incredible.

"Hi, Jazz?" came into Lisha's ear. It sounded like a young guy's voice. "This is way cool that I'm talking to you, you know? Hey, I got your name tattooed on my arm, you know? Hey, I just wanted to say that whoever is the father of your baby is one lucky dude, you know? And, like, I'd be happy to be the dad. I mean, it would be the best thing that ever happened to me, you know? Like, my friends would think it was so bitchin', you know?"

"Please," Lisha said out loud. "I refuse to transcribe this. It's too stupid."

"The girl on this tape wants to have a sex-change operation so she can father Jazz's baby," Chelsea announced. "She said her friends all agree that it would be worth it."

"We should introduce her to the guy on my tape," Lisha said, coughing again. She'd been out of work for two days, and now back at work for two, but she still felt awful. She couldn't seem to get rid of her cough. She popped a cough drop into her mouth and pressed fast forward on her tape.

"Hi, Jazz. My name is Winnie Theyah Pooh. Get it? Winnie the Pooh? I swear to God. I hate my parents for naming me that. My parents suck. I think you should do a show about parents who suck—"

"Yeah, great idea," Lisha said sarcastically. She pressed fast forward again. A low, male voice spoke through her headphones. "Hi, Jazz. Listen, if this is the only way I can get hold of you, so be it. You know who this is. I've got the photos of you, babe. And if you don't do the right thing, the whole world is going to see them real soon."

Lisha paused the tape. "I think someone just threatened Jazz on this tape," she told Chelsea in amazement. "Like he's trying to blackmail her, or something."

"Save it, then, so Her Trashiness can hear it," Chelsea advised.

"Yeah," Lisha agreed. She pressed the proper buttons to save the tape. "It was something about photos of her."

"Who could blackmail Jazz with photos?" Nick asked. "She already posed naked for *Playboy*." He looked over at Chelsea. "And no, I don't own a copy of the magazine, okay?"

Chelsea smiled. "You read my mind." She checked her watch. "Jazz will be on any minute."

Lisha looked up at the overhead monitor, which showed Demetrius warming up the audience before the live show would begin.

"She's not gonna say it's my baby, Chels," Nick said from his computer next to Lisha. "She can't."

"Jazz can do anything." Chelsea licked her lips anxiously.

Lisha shook her head. What a predicament. Nick—who looked a lot like Brad Pitt—had dated Jazz before he'd gotten involved with Chelsea. And now Jazz was pregnant. Jazz claimed she and Nick had slept together. Nick said it was a lie. But Chelsea had told Lisha how one night when Nick had been with Jazz, he had passed out from a combination of beer and cold medicine. And Jazz claimed that that night, they had—

But this couldn't be true.

Still, Jazz was pregnant.

Lisha sighed. *Who knows what the truth is?* she thought. *Chelsea is crazed for Nick. When you're that crazy for a guy, he can make you believe anything.*

Just like Harley.

"There's Jazz," Chelsea said, interrupting Lisha's thoughts. "Turn it up."

Lisha pressed the volume on the remote control, since she was sitting closest to it. The audience was applauding wildly as Jazz walked onto the stage.

"She is so gorgeous," Chelsea said with a sigh.

"Way too obvious," Nick stated firmly.

"You didn't used to think so," Chelsea pointed out.

"Yeah, well, live and learn, okay?" Nick shrugged.

Chelsea looked back at Jazz on the monitor. "Okay, so she's obvious. But she's still awesome looking."

It was true. Jazz, who claimed to be the love child of Rod Stewart, was even better looking than Jenny McCarthy—everyone said so. Only nineteen years old, tall, thin, and voluptuous, with long, straight blond hair, she had been picked by *People* magazine as one of the most beautiful women in the world.

And she was just so outrageous. At the moment she had on a tiny, slinky, multicolored minidress with the middle cut out, which bared her J-shaped navel ring.

"If she's pregnant, it's the world's smallest baby," Lisha commented, staring at Jazz's flat stomach on the monitor.

"It's probably a big scam." Nick frowned in disgust. "She's probably not even really—"

"Shhh," Chelsea said.

"Hey all," Jazz said easily to her audience. "Welcome to my show. Today's the day you all have been waiting for—when I finally name the father of my baby."

"It's me, Jazz!" a guy in the audience yelled out. "I love you!"

Jazz smiled. "I love you, too," she said. "Of course, that is utterly meaningless. But people say it all the time, don't they? 'Love ya! Mean it!'" she added mockingly. "I mean, it's just so . . . so *trashy*, isn't it?"

The audience applauded their agreement. Lisha knew that out of camera range an applause sign was blinking on and off, telling the audience what to do.

"So, what is love, anyway?" Jazz continued. "Today my guests are teen couples who were once in love, but now one of them hates the other, and one of them is still in love. One question is, just how far will the person who's still in love go to get back the person who used to love them?"

The camera came in tight on Jazz's face. "And the other question is, who is the father of my baby? And do I still love him? You'll get the answer at the end of today's show. Love ya! Mean it! How *trashy* it is!"

They went to a commercial.

"I heard about this show," Lisha said. "I think Karma did some work on it. Jazz is going to see how far people will debase themselves for love. It's sick."

"It's Jazz," Nick said, pushing some hair behind his ear. "It's *Trash*."

"I don't know what you ever saw in her," Lisha told Nick, coughing again.

"You really should see a doctor about your cough," Chelsea told Lisha. "At least *Trash* gives us health insurance. It won't cost you anything."

"It's just a cough," Lisha insisted. "No biggie."

"It's almost time, kiddies!" a lilting male voice caroled from the doorway. It was Winston, Jazz's handsome, dreadlocked, Jamaican assistant. "You ready to become world-famous, Nick?"

"It's not my baby, man," Nick protested. "I keep telling you that."

"Yah, man." Winston rolled his eyes. "Keep saying it and maybe you'll start to believe it." He ducked out of the room, laughing.

"I could get to hate that guy," Nick commented darkly.

"Jazz is back on," Chelsea said.

They all returned their attention to the monitor.

34

"My first couple is—"

"Lisha?"

It was Roxanne, standing in the doorway. The cast on her huge foot (a memento of the day she'd been shot on national television) was now down to an Ace bandage. Roxanne wore a lavender silk suit with a very short skirt, and she had matching lavender material wrapped around her Ace bandage.

"Yes?"

"In my office, on the double," Bigfoot barked.

"I'm in the middle of transcribing—"

"Now," Roxanne said, turning on her good foot.

Lisha followed the producer to her office. Roxanne threw a bunch of files at her. "File these."

"You had me come down here now to *file*?" Lisha asked, coughing.

"You missed two days of work and my filing is way behind," Bigfoot said.

"But I was watching—"

"Your job is not to watch the show, Bishop," Roxanne snapped. "It's to slave for me. Get it?"

"You mean work," Lisha corrected her. "Work for the show."

"No. I meant slave for me. And don't ever correct me again. Your work here is slipping, you know. Now, get to it." Roxanne limped out of the office.

"What a witch," Lisha said under her breath. "I guess she's starting to hate me as much as she hates Chelsea."

Lisha began to file. The pile of papers she had to file was huge. She had no idea how much time had passed when she heard a commotion outside the office. Someone was running in the corridor. Voices were loud.

Lisha stuck her head out the door. Brian Bassinger, the executive producer's nephew who delivered the mail, was standing there with Shyanne, Barry's secretary on loan from Sumtimes, who looked just like a brunette Anna-Nicole Smith.

"What's up?" Lisha asked.

"Didn't you hear?" Shyanne asked Lisha.

"If I had heard, why would I be asking you what's going on?" Lisha asked with a cough.

"Jazz just fainted on the air. They've called an ambulance," Brian said.

Lisha ran down the hall and quickly made her way to the studio. The guard at the stage door wouldn't let her in.

"But I work here," she protested.

"So do I," the guard said. "No one gets in except the paramedics."

A crowd of *Trash* employees stood outside the door to the studio, talking in hushed voices, waiting to see what would happen.

Alan came up behind Lisha. Lisha turned to him. "Did you see it happen?"

Alan nodded. "I was watching on the monitor upstairs. Jazz had this guy dress up in a dog's costume and get on all fours and bark to get back the girl he loves. One minute, she was ragging on him for going so low, and the next minute, she just keeled over."

"Make way, make way," the paramedics called as they came bustling in with a stretcher.

"Right through here," the guard said, opening the door to the studio. Lisha rushed in with Alan, and stood in the back of the studio, watching.

The cameras were on a still-passed-out Jazz while Roxanne stood next to her, milking the moment for everything it was worth.

"Jazz is pale and unresponsive," Roxanne was saying, facing camera one. "This is not a publicity stunt. We don't know how serious it is. It could be grave. Ah, here come the paramedics."

"Jeez, Bigfoot is actually making this into a *Trash* live moment," Alan told Lisha with disgust.

The cameras swung to take in the paramedics as they loaded Jazz onto the stretcher and began to take her vital signs.

"Stay with the stretcher," Roxanne called to the camera crew. They followed Jazz and the paramedics as they headed for the door of the studio.

Just as they were about to exit the studio, a small voice rose from the stretcher. "Wait!"

"Jazz!" the studio audience gasped together.

"Put me down," she told the paramedics imperiously.

"But, Jazz—" a young, Hispanic paramedic began.

"Put me down or I sue you," Jazz commanded.

They put her down.

Jazz struggled to sit up. "Is the camera on me?"

"Of course," Roxanne called to her.

Jazz faced the camera. It zoomed in close on her face.

"Pregnant women faint sometimes," she said. "At least that's what I had heard. Now I know it's true."

"We love you, Jazz!" someone in the audience yelled out.

"Yeah, like our couples today love each other," Jazz managed, still sounding weak. "It's all so meaningless, isn't it? I mean, what difference could it make to any of you if I tell you who the father of my baby is? What if he hates me now? What if I hate him? Would he dress up in a dog's costume and bark to get me back?"

The camera swung to the guy on stage in the dog's costume. He grinned and gave a big thumbs-up sign.

"He's too stupid to even look embarrassed," Lisha noted to Alan.

The camera swung back to Jazz. "I mean, how *Trash*y can you get, huh, gang? And I am the queen of *Trash,* as you know. So, who's the king of *Trash*? Who is the father of my baby?"

Everyone in the studio waited, hushed.

Jazz smiled. "Here's what you've all been waiting to hear, you *Trashy* world, you. The father of my baby is . . . Nick Shaw."

"Nick, how does it feel to have the most beautiful girl in the world pregnant with your baby?"

"Look this way, Nick!"

"Are you and Jazz going to get married?"

"Do you think your baby will be more famous than Madonna's kid?"

Lisha and Chelsea watched from their taxi as Nick stood outside the offices of *Trash*, surrounded by journalists and photographers.

"He looks like he's going to kill someone," Chelsea said anxiously as the taxi inched toward the scene on the street.

"Pull up right in front of the building," Lisha told the taxi driver.

"Sorry, sweetheart, no can do," the taxi driver said around the thick cigar he was smoking.

"Why not?" Chelsea asked.

41

"I'll never get outta there," the driver said. "Time is money, babe."

Lisha pulled a twenty-dollar bill out of her purse and waved it at the taxi driver. "Here's money for your time . . . *babe*," she added derisively. "Now, put out the stogie and pull up in front of the building."

"Yes, ma'am," the driver said in a mocking voice. He managed to wedge the taxi in between a van from Channel 4 and a car from NY1 television.

Lisha stuck her head out the window of the taxi.

"Nick!" she called. "Over here!"

Nick's eyes scanned the crowd, finally lighting on Lisha and Chelsea in the taxi. With a look of relief, he ran to them, the crowd of paparazzi following. He got in the taxi and slammed the door. "You guys just saved my butt."

"Nick—"

"Are you Jazz's boy-toy, Nick?" a reporter called.

"Let's get out of here," Chelsea said, reaching for Nick's hand.

"Where to?" the driver asked, turning around in the seat to get a good look at Nick.

"Not home," Lisha said quickly. "They'll follow us."

At that moment Sky dashed out of the *Trash* offices and saw them in the taxi. He ran over and climbed into the front seat, slamming the door behind him. "Brooklyn," he told the driver. "Coney Island Avenue. Sheepshead Bay—"

"I ain't going to—"

"You can't turn the fare down, it's illegal," Sky pointed out. "Now hurry up before the vultures follow us."

Already the reporters were hurrying to their vehicles to chase the taxi.

"They'll never catch Artie Weintraub," the taxi driver said, squealing off. "Eat my dust, vultures!"

"I feel like I'm living in some bizarre parallel universe," Nick said, throwing his head back against the seat. "How could Jazz do this to me?"

Chelsea stared at him. "She must really be in love with you."

"Chels, that is a total crock," Nick said earnestly. "She's just ticked off because you and I are together. And she'll do or say anything for publicity." He leaned forward so he could see Sky in the front seat. "I don't know where we're going in Brooklyn, man, but thanks."

"My cousin's," Sky said. "They'll never follow us there."

Lisha turned to look behind them. Two vans and one car were following their taxi. "Want to bet?"

"It doesn't matter," Sky assured them. "You'll see."

Lisha coughed. "We seem to have this knack for attracting the press, huh?"

"I'd like to kill Jazz, I really would," Nick said, shaking his head.

"Once she gives birth, they'll do a DNA test that will prove you aren't the father," Sky said. "It will prove that, won't it?"

"Yes, it will," Nick snapped. "No way did I have sex with her that one night when I passed out from cold medicine. She's just pulling another one of her scams!"

"She's a genius at it, you have to admit," Lisha said, coughing again.

"I really wish you'd see a doctor about that cough," Chelsea said.

"Yes, Mom," Lisha replied dutifully. "Hey, Chelsea and I talked to Karma right after lunch," she said, leaning toward the front seat. "She sounded so much better."

"We were supposed to go see her tonight," Nick said with disgust. "But I'm not dragging a hundred reporters to the hospital."

"We'll see her," Sky promised.

"Yeah, how you going to arrange that without our escorts?" Lisha asked.

"You'll see." Looking smug, Sky folded his arms.

"Hey, listen, I ain't no eavesdropper, but did I hear right?" the cabbie asked, looking at Nick through his rearview mirror. "You're the father of Jazz Stewart's baby?"

"No!" Nick insisted.

"So why is there a parade behind me, then?" the cabbie asked. "They just like your looks?"

"Look, it's really none of your business," Lisha told him. "Could you just drive, please?"

"Hey, I speak fluent English, I know all five boroughs like the back of my hand, and I happen to own this cab. So show me a little respect!"

An hour or so later they reached Sheepshead Bay, and Sky directed the driver to his cousin's house. Lisha looked behind them—only one car and one van were following them. She knew Sky had grown up in a working-class neighborhood in Brooklyn, that his dad was a tech-union official. And so she was shocked when the cab pulled into a private road blocked by a gate, which clearly led to some kind of an estate. To the left of the gate was a black iron box that looked like an intercom.

Sky got out and spoke into the box. "Hey, it's me," he said. "And send Jarman down here so the leeches who followed us can't get in, okay? Don't open the gate until he gets here." He got back into the front seat of the car.

Lisha just stared at him. "Why do I have a feeling that some really huge mansion is just down this private road?"

Sky grinned at her. "You're so perceptive."

"I guess your cousins are kind of rich, huh?" Chelsea ventured.

"Kind of," Sky said.

"I don't suppose they plan to leave you their fortune," Lisha said. "Because if they do, I'm madly in love with you."

45

"I'm in love with you, too, buddy," the cabbie put in.

A black sedan drove toward them from the private road. The gate opened. A muscular, balding, middle-aged man in jeans got out, pressed a button, and the gate opened.

"Open sesame," the cabbie said, driving through. The gate closed behind him, stopping the press van and car from entering.

The cab rolled to a stop near the man. Sky lowered his window. The man stuck his head into the car. "Hey, Sky, long time no see."

"How ya doin', Jarman?" Sky asked. "These are my friends."

"Not me," the cabbie said. "I'm the designated driver and the meter's running."

"Yeah, well, drive on up to the house, designated driver," Jarman told him, " 'cause I'm the head of security here." He got back into the black car and followed them slowly up the private road.

"Whoa," Lisha breathed, when the house finally came into view. It was huge and modern, with jutting angles made of glass that reflected the early-evening sun.

"Make yourself at home, Sky," Jarman said cheerfully when the group got out of the taxi. He leaned into the driver's-side window and asked, "What's the damage?" Then he paid the taxi bill, peeling money off a fat wad of bills.

"Why do I feel like I'm in a movie right now?" Chelsea asked.

They walked into the house. The front hall was huge, with a forest-green marbled floor. The ceiling was three stories high. "So, just out of curiosity, how close are you to these cousins?" Nick asked, looking around.

"Come on," was all Sky said, not answering Nick's question. He led them down some stairs, into a huge family room. The fireplace was made from the same forest-green marble as the front-hall floor. The green carpet was thick and plush. A large-screen TV stood against the wall. An old-fashioned jukebox gleamed in the corner. Next to that was a soda fountain, complete with silver spigots. Through a wall of glass, Lisha could see a huge, gleaming swimming pool built to look like a lake, surrounded by craggy rocks and hanging branches. A small waterfall cascaded into the middle of it.

"This is too much!" Lisha exclaimed. She looked over at Sky. "I have a feeling we don't know you as well as we thought we knew you."

"Yeah, you do," Sky said, sounding uncomfortable. "I just happen to have some wealthy ex-relatives. And I figured Nick would be safe here."

"*Ex*-relatives?" Chelsea asked.

"My dad's first wife's family," Sky explained. "So I'm not really related to them. But they're cool."

"Glad to hear it," a female voice said. They all turned around. A really cute girl walked into the room. She looked about twenty, with long, straight, red hair, huge green eyes, and a petite, yet voluptuous figure. She wore a pair of white shorts and a white bra top, and carried a tennis racquet in her hand.

"Hi, Fawn," Sky said.

She came over to him and kissed him softly on the lips. "I haven't seen you in forever," she said, wrapping her arms around his neck.

"Ah, kissing cousins, I see," Nick observed with a smirk.

Chelsea nudged her elbow into his side.

"Fawn, these are my friends—Nick, Chelsea, and Lisha," Sky said, gently unwrapping Fawn's arms from around his neck.

Fawn studied Lisha intently. "So . . . you're Lisha."

"Last time I heard."

Fawn stared at her. "He said you were funny. And pretty. And you are."

"True," Lisha said, hoping she sounded cooler than she felt.

Who is that? she wondered. *And why did she kiss Sky on the lips like that?*

"I just beat Daddy in two sets," Fawn announced. "He's up taking a shower—he and Mom are going to some boring thing at the club. He'll be glad to see you, Sky." She smiled at the group. "My father says Sky and I should get married and have gorgeous babies together!"

"So why don't you?" Lisha asked sharply.

Fawn gave her a cool look. "Maybe we will." She tucked her hand through Sky's arm. "So, what brings you here, cuz?"

Sky quickly explained what had just happened on the air.

Fawn's eyes grew wide. She looked at Nick. "You're the father of—"

"I'm not," Nick said quickly. "Jazz is lying."

"Really?" Fawn asked. "How sordid! Wait until I tell all my friends."

"Could you please not tell anyone?" Sky asked.

"You're no fun at all." Fawn pouted. "To repay me, you're going to have to take me to my friend's party tomorrow night."

"Sorry, Fawn, but hanging out with fifteen-year-olds is not my idea of a good time."

"You're only eighteen," Fawn returned, tossing her hair off her face. "I'll get you to change your mind. I'm going to change. Make yourselves at home." She kissed Sky again on the lips, and left.

"She's *fifteen*?" Lisha asked incredulously when Fawn was out of earshot.

Sky nodded. "And she's looked like that since she was twelve. You could say she's kind of precocious. Who's hungry?"

"How long do we have to stay here?" Lisha asked irritably.

Chelsea gave her a strange look.

"Well, I had stuff to do at home," Lisha explained.

I'm not about to tell them all how jealous that girl made me feel, Lisha thought to herself. *But that's crazy. I'm going out with Alan. Not Sky. I don't even* like *Sky!*

I'm such a liar.

"Actually, I was thinking that we could all spend the night here," Sky said. "It's cool with my cousins—I already asked. And it's Friday, No *Trash* tomorrow. And Nick is safe from the vultures here."

"How could we possibly bear hanging out in this dump?" Chelsea asked with a laugh.

"I know, it's a sacrifice," Sky agreed solemnly.

"You sure it's okay?" Chelsea asked.

"Absolutely," Sky said. He flipped a switch and the sounds of Eric Clapton filled the room.

"Fawn says you kids wanna barbecue." They all looked up to see Jarman, who had silently entered the room. "I'll get it taken care of."

"Does he . . . live here?" Nick asked.

"He's Frank's—that's Fawn's dad—he's Frank's best friend."

"Oh," Chelsea said. "But he works as chief—"

"I'll explain some other time," Sky cut in. "So, I guess we're having a barbecue." He began to unbutton his shirt.

"You planning to barbecue naked?" Nick asked archly.

"I plan to take a dip in that pool out there," Sky said. "There are bathing suits in every size in the cabanas. Last one in has to kiss Bigfoot!"

• • •

"I could get used to living like this," Lisha told Chelsea as she splashed her fingers idly through the crystalline water of the swimming pool.

It was dark now, and the water was illuminated by pools of light emanating from fixtures hidden among the rocks. A couple who had introduced themselves as the Vanderwinks had made and served the barbecue (Fawn explained that they'd worked for her family forever), and sometime after that, Fawn's parents, Frankie and Angela, had shown up dressed to designer perfection, greeting Sky like a long-lost son before they left for the evening.

"Me, too," Chelsea admitted. "Although I can't even imagine being this rich."

"I can," Lisha said. "It would be great." She adjusted a strap on the tiny black bikini she'd found in the cabana. She lay on her back on an oversized float, gazing up at the starry night sky.

"I'm so curious about Sky's cousins," Chelsea said from her float, where she lay on her stomach, her head cradled under her hands. She had chosen a one-piece suit cut low in the back, and covered in yellow daisies. "What do you think Fawn's dad does for a living?"

"Something illegal," Lisha guessed.

"I'm sure that's not true," Chelsea said.

"Who knows?" Lisha replied. "Anyway, one thing I know for sure is that Fawn is dangerous." She lifted her head and took in the sight of the girl, sitting at the edge of the pool, her toes dangling in the water. She had on a pink-and-white bikini with a tiny top. Nick was sitting on one side of her, Sky on the other, and they were both laughing at something Fawn had just said. Fawn kept finding reasons to touch Sky.

"She's just a kid," Chelsea said.

"Oh yeah, right, some kid," Lisha snorted. The snort caused her to break into a hacking cough. "I sure wish I could get rid of this."

"I'm telling you, Lish, you need to go to the doctor about that," Chelsea insisted. "Maybe you need antibiotics or something!"

"Yeah, yeah," Lisha said, brushing her off.

"Don't 'yeah, yeah' me," Chelsea said. "If Karma was here, she'd whine at you until you gave in, and you know it."

Lisha smiled. "True. I really miss her."

"Me, too," Chelsea said. "But Dr. Tucci said she can come home next week. Did I tell you that her parents wheeled her into Janelle's room today?"

"When did she tell you that?"

"When we talked to her from the office," Chelsea explained.

"So what did the little Princess of Mean say to Karma, now that Karma almost died saving her sorry butt?" Lisha asked.

"Karma said Janelle said thank you, which I guess is pretty good, coming from Janelle."

"Big deal."

"Then she said she wanted to be alone, and Karma should leave!"

"Now, that sounds like Janelle." Lisha felt hands lifting one side of her raft, and while she struggled to keep her balance the hands managed to dump her into the pool. She came up sputtering to face a laughing Sky. "That was so not funny!"

"Oh yeah, it was," Sky said. "You look cute wet."

"You don't," Lisha retorted.

"Now, now, kids," Chelsea said, laughing.

Sky splashed some water at Lisha. "Want to go for a walk? You should see the flower garden—it's really beautiful."

"I thought you were baby-sitting." Lisha cocked her head toward Fawn.

"She's no baby," Sky said.

"Yuh, I noticed," Lisha replied. "I thought she was in college when I first saw her."

"Everyone says that," Sky said. "So, walk?"

"She's crazy about you, you know."

Sky raised his eyebrows and held his hand over his heart. "Could it be . . . are you . . . jealous?"

"No, I'm not jealous," Lisha spat at him. "Why would I be jealous?"

"Hey, Sky, could you come put some oil on my back?" Fawn called to him.

"It's nighttime, Fawn," he called back. "You can't get a tan now."

Fawn smiled. "I know."

Lisha made a noise in her throat. "She's really fifteen? She's scary."

"So, how about that walk?"

"Okay." Lisha turned to Chelsea. "Make Nick feel better while we're gone."

"It looks like Fawn is cheering him up," Chelsea observed darkly. Fawn had her hand on Nick's biceps, and was leaning toward him, telling him something, her face animated.

"Save him while you can," Sky suggested. He jumped out of the pool and reached a hand down to help Lisha out. Then he wrapped her in an oversized white terry-cloth robe.

"Sky, I really wanted you to hear my new CD," Fawn said, running over to them.

"I'll hear it later," Sky told her.

Fawn's eyes shot daggers at Lisha. "Why, what are the two of you going to do now?"

"We're going for a walk," Sky said easily.

"Can I come?" Fawn asked.

"No," Sky said, ruffling her hair. "You can't."

"I hate it when you do that!" Fawn swatted at his hand. "I'm not a little kid anymore, Sky!"

"I can see that," he admitted.

"No, you can't see that," Fawn said. She raised her chin defiantly. "But you will. Soon." She turned on her heel and went back to where Nick had been joined by Chelsea.

Lisha slipped on her sandals, and she and Sky headed down a cobblestone path, through manicured bushes and trees.

"You know Fawn is in love with you, don't you?" Lisha asked quietly.

Sky laughed. "She's just practicing on me. Her parents don't even let her date yet."

"I don't know—" Lisha began.

"Look, I don't want to talk about Fawn, okay?" He took her hand.

They kept walking until they reached a gladelike space that bloomed with a riot of flowers. The beauty of it took Lisha's breath away. "It's unbelievable!" she cried.

"I know," Sky said. "I used to love to come here when I was a kid, just to think."

Lisha looked at him. "That sounds like something Alan would do."

Sky raised his eyebrows at her. "Look, I know I'm not this deep poet like Alan is, okay? But that doesn't mean I never think."

"I didn't mean it like that—"

"Yeah, you did," Sky said. He sat on the stone bench, under a plant with red-and-orange flowers.

Lisha sat down next to him. "I just meant that I think of you as being—I don't know— physical. And Alan as being cerebral."

"Well, I don't fit into a little box, and neither does Alan," Sky said.

"I know," she replied, her voice low.

They were silent for a moment. The only sound was crickets. Fireflies lit up the sky.

"I used to catch fireflies when I was a kid," Lisha remarked. "In a jar."

"Yeah?"

She nodded. "With Chelsea. Of course, then she always got afraid that they couldn't breathe in there or something, so she always set them free."

Sky smiled. "That sounds like Chelsea."

Lisha smiled, too. "She was the world's greatest best friend when we were kids. She had tons of friends and I . . . well, she was my only friend."

"How come?"

She shrugged. "I was fat. And insecure. Inside my mind I was this rock-and-roll rebel. But I looked like this nerdy little butterball." She looked over at him. "I guess you were always great looking."

"I never think of myself that way."

"Bull," Lisha snorted.

"I look okay," Sky said. "I don't think about it much." He stared at her, and his voice grew soft. "It's hard to picture you as ever being anything except as gorgeous as you are now."

"Take my word for it," she said, looking away from him. "And it was awful."

Gently, Sky touched her chin, and turned her face to his. "Looks aren't such a big deal, Lish."

"Now you sound like Alan again," she said nervously. Just being this close to him made her heart hammer in her chest.

I should get up and leave, she thought to herself. *I should just go. This is dangerous. Really dangerous.*

"Lish—"

She jumped up. "We should go. Don't you think we should go?"

He stood up, too. "We need to talk, Lish—"

"No, we don't," she said firmly. "I'm going out with Alan."

"I know, but—"

"I care about him," Lisha said. "He's the sweetest guy in the world. And he's your roommate. And your friend."

Sky just stared at her.

"Besides, I just remembered that I don't like you," Lisha added quickly.

Sky didn't move.

She couldn't bring herself to look at him, so she stared at her hands. Anywhere but at his face, his eyes, his lips.

God, his lips.

He turned her toward him. "Lisha, I've wanted you forever," he said huskily.

Then his lips were on hers, so softly that she barely felt his kiss. He kissed her again. And again. Until she felt her arms go around his neck, and heard his groan, and even though she knew it was the very, very last thing she should be doing, she pressed her body to his, and everything in the world, for that moment, became Sky.

"I can't believe I did that," Lisha groaned, burying her head in a pillow from the couch.

It was the next morning, and Lisha, Chelsea, Sky, and Nick had arrived home an hour before. The good news was that, per usual, the news hounds had already moved on to another story, so they hadn't been surrounded when they got home. The bad news was that Lisha had passionately made out with Sky the night before, and now, by the light of day, she regretted it big time.

"So, you kissed Sky," Chelsea said from the kitchen, where she was getting some ice cream from the fridge. "It's not the end of the world."

"Believe me, I didn't just casually kiss him," Lisha said. "This was hot. This was more than hot. This was *illegally* hot!"

Chelsea got a spoon from the drawer and sat down with the ice cream. "God, I'm eating ice cream for breakfast. I'm turning into Karma. How could you and I both hurt Alan when we both think so much of him?"

"Because we're terrible people," Lisha said with a sigh. "We have no morals. We should be shot."

"What are you going to do?" Chelsea asked, swallowing some ice cream.

"Pretend last night never happened?" Lisha asked hopefully.

"I doubt it," Chelsea said.

"I don't want a relationship with Sky!" Lisha cried. "I don't!"

Chelsea gave her a look.

"I mean it." Lisha insisted. "He's way too hot for his own good."

"For *your* own good, you mean," Chelsea corrected.

"Very funny."

"I just don't see what your problem is," Chelsea said earnestly. "I mean, Sky is a great guy. And the two of you have this intense thing for each other—"

"We do not."

"You're lying," Chelsea looked her friend in the eye. "You do. I don't know why you want to keep running away from it."

"Because it's too scary, okay?" Lisha exploded. "Can't you understand how after Harley I'd want to feel safe?"

Chelsea was silent for a moment. "I can. You're right. I didn't think about that."

Lisha rubbed the bridge of her nose, where a headache was forming. "Besides, I really do care about Alan. I don't want to hurt him."

"I didn't want to hurt him, either," Chelsea said with a sigh. "But I did. Are you going to tell Alan what happened?"

"I don't know," Lisha groaned. "I hate myself right about now." She started coughing again. "This stupid cough is driving me nuts!"

There was a knock on the door. Chelsea jumped up. "I hope it's Nick," she said, hurrying to the door.

It was Sky. He grinned when he saw Lisha. "Hey, I know a great place for lunch that has your name on it."

"I'm not hungry," Lisha said.

"Come on, you love to eat," Sky cajoled her.

"No, you're thinking of Karma. You know. Our other roommate. The one who's in the hospital. I hate eating. I never eat."

"Excuse me," Chelsea interrupted. "I think I'll go across the hall and see what Belch is doing." Belch was Nick's beloved dog. Beloved by Nick, anyway.

"Very funny," Lisha called as Chelsea hurried out of the apartment. "Desert me in my hour of need."

Sky came over to Lisha. "You look so cute," he told her, kneeling down next to the couch.

"Look, Sky, can't we just pretend that last night never happened?"

He raised his eyebrows. "Why would I want to do that?"

"Because it was a stupid mistake." Lisha sat up. "Go . . . go work your supposed charm on Fawn, or something."

He studied her. "Is that what you want me to do?"

"Is that what you want to do?" she asked carefully.

Sky stood up. "I'm not into playing games with you, Lish. All I did was ask you out for lunch. Come on. It'll be fun. Nothing heavy, I promise."

"For sure?"

"I'm not even looking for anything heavy," Sky explained.

"What does 'heavy' mean?" Lisha asked.

"Love," he said. "Or commitment."

"Oh, so you just want to hang out and have fun," Lisha said.

"Right," Sky agreed, his face breaking into a smile. "Isn't that what you want?"

I don't know what I want, Lisha admitted silently. *But I can't stop thinking about you. Or dreaming about you. Or imagining what it would be like to—*

Stop that, she ordered herself in her mind. *Think about Alan.*

"What about Alan?" she finally said.

Sky sighed and sat on the end of the couch. "You need to talk with him."

"Not if I don't start seeing you, I don't," Lisha said. "Like I said, last night was a mistake—"

"Did anyone ever point out how exhausting it is to have a conversation with you?" Sky asked. "I don't want to analyze this to death, okay? I don't want to write you a love sonnet. I like you. I care about you. I think you are incredibly hot. Now, are you into it, or not?"

Not. Say you're not. Say it right now, Lisha ordered herself.

"I'm not," she said.

There, she thought *I did it.*

Sky laughed. "You're such a bad liar."

Lisha's face turned red with fury. "And you are an egotistical butthole!"

Sky pulled her up from the couch. His hands went around her narrow waist. He gazed down into her eyes. "Just have lunch with me. There's someplace special I want to take you. And after that, if you decide it's Alan you want, I'll never bother you again."

"Just lunch, huh?"

"Just lunch," he said. "No big deal."

She thought a moment. "Okay," she finally answered. "Why is this place you want to take me to so special?"

Sky grinned. "You'll see."

Lisha's voice could barely be heard over the roar of the plane's engine. Her heart was thudding in her chest. The small runway from which she and Sky had taken off looked like a Band-Aid below them.

"You never told me you had your pilot's license!" Lisha yelled over the noise.

"There's a lot about me you don't know," Sky yelled back from the pilot's seat.

They were in a tiny two-seater plane, with Sky at the controls. When he had driven her to Long Island, to the small, private airstrip, she had no idea in the world that he was about to *fly* her to lunch somewhere.

"Whose plane is this, anyway?"

"Fawn's dad," Sky said. He pushed a button and a gauge in front of them leveled out. "Pretty cool, huh?"

"This really is legal and everything?" Lisha asked nervously.

Sky laughed. "Totally." He picked up the small radio unit and spoke into it. "This is the *Golden Goose,* leveling off at thirteen thousand feet, over."

"You're a-okay on your designated flight plan, *Golden Goose,* over and out," the air-traffic controller called back.

Lisha looked down at the ground. All she could see was the tops of trees, which looked like little, green pinheads stuck in a map of the world. "This is awesome," she admitted.

"Yeah, I know," Sky said. He pushed a button, and the sounds of an old Bruce Springsteen CD filled the cockpit.

An hour later he expertly landed the plane at

a tiny airport, someplace in Connecticut. When they left the plane, a silver Porsche convertible was waiting for them. Sky got in the driver's seat.

"I have a feeling I'm supposed to be dazzled," Lisha said faintly.

"Is it working?" Sky asked as he started the car's purring engine.

"Yeah, basically," she admitted.

Sky drove through the lush countryside until they came to a tiny gold, engraved sign that read JARMAN'S. He turned down the road, and they drove until they came to a stately red-brick building. A uniformed bellboy took the car as Sky jumped out and opened Lisha's car door.

"I should have worn something other than jeans," Lisha commented, looking down at her favorite faded jeans with the holes in the knees. With them, she wore a tiny, sheer black crepe blouse that bared her stomach and hinted at the black, lacy bra she wore underneath.

"You look great," Sky assured her as he ushered her into the restaurant.

A tuxedoed maître d' seated them at a table on the garden patio, put down their menus, and silently left them alone.

Lisha opened her menu, but she didn't look at it. "Aren't you the guy who told me 'just lunch, no big deal'?"

"Well, we're about to have lunch," Sky pointed out.

"And you call this no big deal?"

He shrugged. "I might be trying to impress you."

"It might be working," she admitted. "But doesn't this restaurant have the same name as the guy at Fawn's house—"

"I always said you were quick," Sky said.

"Does he own it? And how come Fawn's dad lets you take his plane? And what does—"

"I thought we weren't going to talk," Sky interrupted.

"Yeah, well, that's when I thought we were going to some local dive for burgers. What's the deal, Sky?"

Sky put his menu down. "It's like this. Fawn's dad is a great guy. He thinks of me as the son he never had. He's the one who taught me to fly."

"And Jarman?" Lisha prompted.

"Jarman saved Fawn's dad's life in Vietnam," Sky explained. "Fawn's dad owns this restaurant. He named it after his bud."

Lisha thought for a moment. "And Fawn's dad wants you and Fawn to get together, doesn't he? As in married. So you can *really* be his son someday."

"Yeah," Sky admitted.

"Which means that Fawn's dad would not be jumping for joy to know that you used his plane and his Porsche to take another girl to the restaurant that he owns."

Sky scratched his chin. "Fawn is like a sister to me—"

"Some sister."

"She's just a kid—"

"Oh, yeah," Lisha snorted.

"Why are we talking about Fawn?" Sky asked. "Can you please answer me that?"

"Because all of this"—Lisha's hand swept through the air—"all of this is because of Fawn's dad. And I have a feeling it's because he really hopes you and his little girl will end up happily-ever-after."

Sky shook his head no. "Fawn is only fifteen, Lish. And her dad loves me, whether or not Fawn and I ever get together."

"Are you sure about that?"

"Positive." He reached for her hand. "Now, can we talk about something else?"

"Okay," Lisha agreed. She opened her menu. "What's good to eat at this dive?"

Karma's hospital bed was cranked into an upright position. She sat there, her hair on top of her head in a messy ponytail, wearing a Ralph Lauren designer peignoir set in burgundy-and-orange paisley. Lisha and Chelsea sat in chairs they had pulled up to her bed.

It was that evening, and Lisha had just finished telling Karma about Sky's cousin's house, and about her date with him that afternoon.

"Wait, you're telling me that Sky is *rich?*" Karma asked incredulously.

"His ex-cousins are rich," Chelsea corrected.

"Well, if Fawn's daddy—or Fawn, for that matter, has anything to say about it, one day Sky will be related to them by marriage," Lisha said.

"You should see this girl, Karma," Chelsea said. "Fifteen going on thirty."

"And she wants Sky bad," Lisha added.

"Hey, now that I know Sky is rich, *I* want him bad!" Karma said in her characteristic nasal whine. "Who knew?" She waggled her fingers at her friends. "Whaddaya think of the manicure?" Her fingernails were painted a sparkling, deep blue.

"Very you," Chelsea said.

"I know," Karma agreed, admiring her nails. "It's Chanel nail polish. I love it. Janelle was in here this afternoon. I offered to paint hers for her but her face turned darker than the nail polish."

"I don't know how you can stand her," Lisha said.

Karma shrugged. "She's my sister."

"No," Lisha corrected her. "*We're* your white Asian sisters. She's just . . . just some identical accident of birth."

"White Asian sisters, I love that! Anyway, she's getting sprung from here soon," Karma said. "So am I, by the by."

"When?" Lisha asked.

"Early next week," Karma answered. "Although I'm not so anxious to leave. I mean, I have this one doctor who is to die for. He's Jewish, too. I keep hoping he'll ask me out."

"But you're in love with Demetrius!" Lisha exclaimed.

"True," Karma said. "I didn't say I'd actually *go*. I just need an ego boost." She turned to Chelsea. "So, what's up with you and Mr. Canada Slacker?"

"Nick." Chelsea sighed. "I told you that Jazz announced on the air that she's pregnant with his baby—"

"That means exactly nothing," Karma decreed. "We're talkin' Jazz, here."

"I know," Chelsea agreed. "But it's still hard."

"I'm telling you," Karma said, "it's all gonna come out that she was lying. So don't let her manipulate you, or come between you and Nick. That's exactly what she's trying to do."

Lisha grinned at Karma. "God, we miss you so much."

"There's just no one else like you, Karma."

"Yeah, I know," Karma agreed. "Well, there's someone who looks like me—"

"Janelle can't shine your designer pumps," Chelsea insisted.

Karma made a face. "And she's so . . . so Bass loafers. How did I end up with a twin with no fashion sense? Hey, I just remembered something. Is Nick still going with Jazz to the Rock of Ages Awards next Saturday?"

"I haven't had the nerve to bring it up," Chelsea admitted. "The press will go crazy photographing Jazz out with the supposed father of her baby."

"So, tell him not to go," Lisha advised. "If Nick loves you, he'll understand how you feel."

"Maybe I should," Chelsea said. "I'll think about it. I know! We'll give a coming-home party for Karma next Saturday! Nick will have to come to that instead of going to the awards with Jazz."

"A party sounds fab," Karma said. "But ask him not to go with her, no matter what."

"You look gorgeous," came a masculine voice from the doorway.

Lisha and Chelsea turned around. Demetrius stood in the doorway, carrying a huge bouquet of summer flowers.

"Look, a Greek god arrives with a floral tribute," Karma whined.

"For a goddess," Demetrius intoned, smiling and approaching the bed. He leaned over and kissed Karma. "How can you look so cute when you're a patient in the hospital?"

"Long-term beauty maintenance," Karma said seriously. "How do you manage to look like you just stepped off the cover of a romance novel?"

"Long-term maintenance," Demetrius replied, laughing. He gazed down at her, his face suffused with love. Gently, he leaned over and cupped his huge hand around the line of her jaw. "How ya doing?" he asked tenderly.

"Well, we'd better be going," Lisha said, pushing out of her chair. Chelsea got up, too.

"You two don't have to leave on my account," Demetrius protested.

"It's okay, we were leaving, anyway." Chelsea leaned over and kissed Karma. So did Lisha. "So, we'll come see you tomorrow after work, okay?"

"Okay," Karma agreed.

"Is there anything you want us to bring?" Lisha asked.

Karma thought a moment. "A huge pastrami sandwich on rye from the Carnegie Deli."

"You got it," Lisha replied.

She and Chelsea walked out of the hospital and to the nearest subway stop, where they were lucky enough to have an express train show up almost immediately.

"Demetrius is so crazy about her," Lisha commented over the sound of the train.

"So?" Chelsea responded. "You've got two guys crazy about you. What are you going to do about that, anyway?"

Lisha leaned her head back. "I don't know."

"But you admit you have feelings for Sky—"

"Wanting to jump his bones is not the same as having feelings for him."

"Meaning you're only into him sexually?" Chelsea asked, wrinkling her face. "You'd be so ticked off if a guy said that about you!"

"True."

"Anyway, I think you're lying. I think you're into Sky a lot."

Lisha nervously turned the simple opal ring she wore around on her finger. "Maybe."

"It isn't fair to Alan if you don't say something."

"I know."

By the time they got back to their apartment building, it was almost ten o'clock. When they walked in, Antoine, their doorman, was, for once, actually on duty.

"Hi," he said, looking up from his racing form. "Hey, girls, I got a great tip on a pacer, if you're interested."

Antoine had a serious weakness for betting on harness-racing horses.

"I don't think you're supposed to be offering gambling tips to the tenants," Chelsea pointed out.

"Yeah," Antoine admitted. "But I was just trying to share the wealth."

As the girls went up in the slow, ancient elevator, Chelsea looked over at Lisha. "Maybe you should talk to Alan tonight."

"I'm too tired," Lisha said.

"Well, don't put it off too long—"

"Don't push me!" Lisha exclaimed. Chelsea looked hurt. "I'm sorry, Chels. I'm just . . . I'm confused."

"It's okay," Chelsea said. "I probably just feel guilty because Alan was in love with me once, and . . . well, I didn't handle it very well."

The elevator stopped at their floor, and they got out. "There is no good way to handle it," Lisha said, getting out the keys to their apartment as they walked down the hall. "And I don't even know what I want to do about everything! I mean, just because Sky whisks me off in an airplane, just because Sky is so darned sexy that I can't think straight—"

"I heard that."

Lisha looked up. Fawn was standing just outside the guys' apartment, her arms folded, her face furious.

"What are you doing here?" Lisha asked in surprise.

"Visiting Sky," Fawn said. She took a step toward Lisha. "There's something you need to know."

"What's that?" Lisha asked warily.

Fawn put her face up close to Lisha's. "Sky is mine. Do you hear me? Mine. And you'll never, ever get him."

Fawn, honey," Lisha said, her voice oozing sweetness, "I think you've been watching too many soap operas. Do the words *Days of Our Lives* ring a bell with you?"

"I'm totally serious," Fawn said, standing her ground.

Chelsea reached out to touch the younger girl. "Look, Fawn, this isn't some kind of game—"

"No one asked you," Fawn said rudely. She pushed her long, red hair off her face, then her eyes met Lisha's again. "I think you should invite me in so we can talk."

Lisha laughed. "I don't think so. I don't even like you."

"I don't like you, either," Fawn said. "But you should invite me in, anyway."

"Look, you're visiting Sky, right?" Lisha asked, losing whatever patience she still had. "So go visit him. And get out of my face."

With that, she pushed past Fawn and un-locked the door to their apartment.

"You'll be sorry, Lisha," Fawn called as Lisha and Chelsea entered their apartment.

"Nighty-night," Lisha singsonged, and closed the door on Fawn's angry face. She turned to Chelsea. "Do you believe that kid?"

"She's amazing," Chelsea agreed. "What's she doing visiting Sky this late at night, any-way? How could her parents allow it?"

Lisha flicked on the light and threw herself on the couch. "I guess when you were fifteen you were home by eight o'clock on the week-ends, huh?" she teased.

Chelsea got a Coke from the fridge. "Well, my mom was kind of . . . overprotective, I guess." She sighed, and sat in the overstuffed chair. "And now the whole world knows why."

Lisha put her hands under her head. "It's still hard for me to believe that your dad actu-ally . . . did what your dad did."

"It's hard for me to believe it, too," Chelsea agreed. Her pinkie finger made a circle on the sweating edge of her Coke can. "Sometimes when I get angry, I mean really angry, I worry that . . . that I'm like him, or something."

Lisha sat up. "Come on, Chels—"

"I'm serious," Chelsea said, still staring at her can of Coke. "What if I am? What if I did something terrible?"

"Chels, something was seriously wrong with

your dad," Lisha said earnestly, leaning forward to look at Chelsea. "You didn't inherit it."

"How do you know?"

"Because I know you," Lisha said. "I've known you forever." She looked thoughtful for a moment. "On the other hand, if you ever have a murderous impulse, you could aim for Fawn—"

"That's not funny!" Chelsea cried, although her lips were twitching with laughter.

"Okay, not Fawn, you're right," Lisha amended. "Bigfoot. Take out Roxanne. That would be great."

There was a knock on their door.

"Oh, great, it's Fawn," Lisha groaned. "Go away!" she yelled toward the door.

Another knock, louder.

Lisha got up and marched to the door. "Look, Fawn—" she began. Only it wasn't Fawn. It was Alan. "Oh, hi," she said guiltily. "I thought you were—"

"Fawn," Alan filled in. "I heard. Listen, can we talk?"

"Gee, Alan, I'm really beat," Lisha said quickly. "Maybe tomorrow—"

"We really need to talk," he said firmly, his eyes boring into hers.

"Yeah," she said softly. "I guess we do."

"Not here, huh?" Alan shoved his hands into the pockets of his jeans. "I'm starting to feel like I'm living on *Melrose Place,* or something. Let's go for a walk."

Lisha turned to Chelsea. "Chels, I'm—"

"I heard," Chelsea said. "See ya."

Lisha grabbed her purse and slung the strap over her shoulder. She and Alan traveled down in the elevator and out to the street in silence.

I don't know what to say to him, she thought. *I don't want to hurt him. And I don't know how I feel.*

"So, what do you think of Fawn?" Lisha managed as they headed down the street.

"She's desperate to be grown up," Alan said.

"Oh, believe me, she's grown up," Lisha remarked.

"No. She's all bluff. She's a little girl playing dress-up. Only the stakes involved are a lot higher than messing up her mommy's cosmetics." He shot her a hard look.

"You hungry?" Lisha asked nervously. "Want to go eat?"

"Not really."

"Me, either."

"Let's go down by the river, huh?"

"Okay," she agreed.

When they reached the Hudson, Lisha could see the moonlight reflecting off the water. Just across the river, she could see the lights of New Jersey. It was a clear night, and the humidity was, for once, low. She took a deep breath. "The air doesn't even stink tonight," she said playfully.

Alan was silent.

Lisha looked at him out of the corner of her

eye. *This is horrible,* she thought. *I want to be anyplace at all right now except here.*

"Well, you wanted to talk," she blurted out, when she couldn't take the silence.

Alan stared out at the water. "I know what's going on."

"What's that?" Lisha asked.

He wouldn't look at her. "You. And Sky."

"There really isn't any me and Sky—"

"Come on, Lish," he interrupted. "This is me you're talking to."

Lisha pushed her feathery bangs off her forehead. She was silent for a long time. "I don't know what to say, Alan."

"I can see that."

She looked over at him. "I'm not in love with Sky."

"You're not?" he asked. He looked confused.

"No," Lisha said.

"Then why did you sleep with him?"

Lisha's mouth fell open. "I *what?*"

"Why did you sleep with him?" Alan asked, hurt straining his voice.

"Did that lowlife say I slept with him?" Lisha yelled. "I'll kill him! He's a damned liar, Alan! I mean it! I should have known he'd do something that low!"

"He didn't tell me about it," Alan said, "so calm down."

"Then what are you talking about?" Lisha asked.

Alan stared at her. "Fawn told me the truth."

Lisha laughed. "You're kidding."

"Do I look like I'm kidding?"

She stared into his hurt eyes. "No, you don't. Alan, Fawn is lying."

"I don't think so," he said.

"Why the hell would you believe her over me?" Lisha asked incredulously.

"Did you go over to Fawn's house last night?" Alan asked.

"Yes," Lisha replied. "With Chelsea and Sky and Nick. To protect Nick from the press."

Alan nodded. "Did you spend the night there last night?"

"What is this, an inquisition?" she asked. "Yeah, we all spent the night there. But that doesn't mean—"

"Did you and Sky go off together? Did you go to the private flower garden with him so the two of you could be alone? Did he say, 'Lisha, I've wanted you forever'? And then he started to kiss you, and then—"

"Stop this!" Lisha cried, shaking. "This is disgusting. Are you telling me that Fawn told you all this?"

"How else would I know?" Alan asked bitterly. "My best friend, Sky, and my girlfriend, Lisha, sure as hell didn't tell me about it."

"Well, how could she know?" Lisha shot back. "Unless she followed us. Unless she was . . . was watching us, like some kind of sick, little—"

"How can you, of all people, be calling her names?"

Lisha put her hands to her head. "This is crazy."

"Yeah, I agree," Alan said. "You think I like having this conversation? You think I like hearing the horrible truth from Fawn, because my friends are lying to me and behind my back they're—"

"Alan, stop," Lisha said, tears in her eyes. "Please. Just stop. I'm sorry I didn't tell you what happened with Sky last night. It's not like I've had a lot of chances to talk with you since then."

Alan sighed. He stared out at the water again. " 'It's better to have loved and lost than never to have loved at all.' You know that one, Lish?"

"You haven't lost—"

"You and Sky are lovers," Alan said bluntly.

"Alan, that isn't true." she insisted. "Fawn is lying about that."

He looked at her. "Is she?"

"Yes."

"The two of you didn't make love in the flower garden last night?"

"No."

"Want to know why Fawn is so upset about seeing you and Sky together?" Alan asked.

"I already know why," Lisha replied. "She has some demented fifteen-year-old idea that Sky is hers."

"She's sleeping with Sky," Alan said.

Lisha laughed. "That's ridiculous."

"I believe her," Alan said.

"Alan, it's all in her head. Sky has no interest in her, except as a sister."

Alan reached down and picked up a stone, and he threw it out at the water. "Is that how you think of me, Lisha? As a brother?"

"I don't know," she admitted. "I care about you—"

"I know that," he said. He smiled his endearing, crooked smile. "First Chelsea, now you. I seem to have a bad habit of falling for women who don't exactly fall for me back."

"Maybe you're just . . . just too *nice,* Alan!" Lisha blurted out.

"Meaning what, that I need to be more of a bastard for women to want me?" Alan asked bitterly. "No, thanks, Lisha. That's not me."

"I know it's not you," she said. She reached out and put her hand on his arm. "It's just that you're a much better person than I am. I never did deserve you."

Alan laughed a low, sad chuckle. "I never know what it means when women tell me that. If I put clichés like that in my writing, I'd never sell a damn thing."

"I'm sorry," Lisha said sincerely.

He nodded. "I know."

"And I'm not sleeping with Sky."

"Yet."

"I'm *not,*" she said firmly. She saw a weathered park bench behind them and headed for it.

"And I'm sure Fawn isn't, either. Sky isn't crazy."

Alan sat with her. "Sky wasn't home when Fawn showed up tonight. She told me a lot of . . . interesting stuff."

"A lot of stupid lies, you mean," Lisha corrected.

"Maybe," Alan said. "But maybe not. For example, did you know that her father thinks of Sky as the son he never had?"

"Sky already told me that," Lisha said defensively.

"Did you know that if Sky marries Fawn, he gets five million dollars?"

Lisha stared at Alan's somber face, illuminated by a dim streetlight. "You're kidding."

"Nope. Five million."

"And if he doesn't marry her?"

"Zip."

Lisha thought for a moment. "Oh, come on, that isn't true. Fawn made that up, just like she lied about—"

"I don't think so, Lisha."

"Why don't you just ask Sky if it's true, then," Lisha challenged.

"Oh, I'm sure he'll tell me the truth," Alan said. "Just like he told me he was after you."

"I'll ask him, then," she decided, getting up.

Alan stood up, too. He smiled sadly at her. "So . . . what about us?"

"I don't know," she said, her voice low.

"I do," Alan said. "It's back to good-buddy Alan."

"It doesn't have to be—"

"Yes, it does," he said with quiet dignity. "I think I missed my era, you know? I feel like Ashley Wilkes. And guys like Nick and Sky are Rhett Butler."

"Oh, Alan—"

He smiled at her. "I won't stop caring about you, Lisha. And you know, I didn't really believe that kid. I'm just, well, kind of jealous."

Lisha felt like crying. "I know." She sniffed back her tears. "I wish you'd hug me."

"Can't do that, Lisha. Not right now," Alan said.

Lisha wanted to reach out to him. She wanted to apologize. She couldn't stand the hurt on his face, nor the knowledge that she had put it there.

"Alan, I—"

She stopped herself. What could she say that she hadn't already said?

Alan reached for her hand. "Come on. Let's go home."

"**I**s anyone missing?" Bigfoot asked Sumtimes as she looked around at the faces of all the staff she had summoned to a meeting in the main conference room first thing Monday morning.

Sumtimes, who shaved her head as a fashion statement, had her bald scalp swathed gypsystyle in a paisley scarf that matched her short, paisley minidress. She looked down at a list on her clipboard, then her face scanned the crowd.

"Everyone's here."

"Good," Roxanne said. She took a seat at the head of the conference table. Then she regally tipped her head at the rest of them.

"I guess that means we can sit, too," Lisha muttered to Chelsea as they pulled out two chairs from the huge, gleaming mahogany conference table.

"There aren't enough seats for everyone," Bigfoot called out loudly. "The interns can stand."

Lisha and Chelsea moved away from the chairs, their faces red with embarrassment. While Roxanne spoke to one of the female associate producers, Lisha leaned close to Chelsea. "Notice anything bizarre about this little gathering?"

"It's all women," Chelsea said, looking around.

Lisha nodded. "Not only that, but every single woman who works for *Trash* is in this room."

"You're right," Chelsea realized. "Except Karma, who's in the hospital."

"And that paralegal what's-her-name who's out on maternity leave," Lisha said. "Now, why would Bigfoot call every woman on staff to a meeting?"

"We're about to find out," Chelsea whispered.

A secretary from billing brought two hard, wooden chairs in for Lisha and Chelsea. Chelsea smiled at her gratefully.

"That was nice," Lisha commented, taking a seat. Chelsea sat, too.

Bigfoot rattled her papers, took a drink of water from a Waterford crystal goblet, and called the meeting to order.

"We're here for a very happy occasion," she said in her usual flat, businesslike voice. "We're here to plan Jazz's baby shower." She shot Chelsea a nasty smile.

Chelsea gasped. Lisha reached for her friend's hand and gave her a reassuring squeeze.

"We're going to give Jazz a surprise baby shower on the air," Bigfoot continued.

"Excuse me," Lisha interjected, "but how is it possible to surprise Jazz on the air when she plans every show?"

Roxanne gave her a scathing look. "Did I somehow indicate that it was time for you to speak?"

Lisha gave Bigfoot a look of disgust.

"Watch it, Bishop," Roxanne said. "I already warned you once." She smiled, though her eyes remained as cold as ice. "So, anyone else object to doing a nice deed for the woman who employs us all?"

The room was silent.

"Funny, I thought you'd see it my way." Roxanne smirked. "Now, what I'm thinking is that we should do a whole sexist, bachelor-party role-reversal thing. We'll have a giant cake. And—I'm really proud of coming up with this idea, I have to tell you—Nick Shaw will jump out of it!"

Chelsea gasped again. Even Sumtimes looked nonplussed. "Uh, Roxanne, maybe that isn't such a good idea . . ." Sumtimes began.

"It happens to be a world-class idea," Roxanne announced frostily.

"But it seems to me that Jazz wouldn't—"

"I'm a lot closer to Jazz than you are," Bigfoot told Sumtimes. "She confides in me."

Sumtimes nodded. "That's great, Roxi, but I still think—"

"Sumtimes," Bigfoot interrupted. "Can it. This was all Jazz's idea."

"I thought you just said it was your idea," a young woman from accounting pointed out.

Roxanne treated her to a scathing look. "I said the *cake* with Nick *in* the cake was my idea."

"If Jazz knows about this, how can it be a surprise?" Lisha asked.

"The *date* is a surprise," Roxanne explained. She eyed Chelsea, her face smirking. "Well, Chelsea, what do you think of our little plan?"

Chelsea raised her chin, her eyes glittering at Roxanne. "Nick is not going to agree to jump out of a cake."

"You don't think so?" Roxanne asked. "Why not? After all, he is the father of Jazz's baby. Why wouldn't he want to keep her happy?"

"He's not the father," Chelsea said, her voice low.

"How do you know?" Roxanne asked, her eyes wide. "Were you there?"

Chelsea's face burned. "No. I wasn't."

"Just because you had a very brief, very little fling with Nick is no reason to get bent out of shape."

"I'm not getting bent out of shape," Chelsea

said slowly. "But what I'm telling you is the truth. Nick isn't the father."

"Yes, he is," Roxanne insisted. "I don't intend to argue this with you, just because you got your little feelings hurt."

Chelsea could feel dozens of pairs of eyes going from Roxanne to her, waiting breathlessly to see what would happen.

"Ignore her," Lisha told Chelsea, her voice low. "Don't fall for her bait."

But Chelsea was too livid to listen. She stood up. Leaning her hands on the conference table, she glared hard at Roxanne. "Nick is not the father of that baby," she repeated. "He never slept with Jazz. It's a big scam."

Roxanne smiled her evil grin. "Oh, I guess lover-boy told you that."

"Nick told me that, yes," Chelsea said, her voice even.

"And you believed that little stud-muffin?" Roxanne hooted. Dutifully, many of the underlings on the staff laughed with her.

"He's not a—"

"Stud-muffin?" Roxanne interrupted. "He's way up there on the hottie-meter. Even I have to admit that."

Lisha could see Chelsea's face turn even redder with anger. Her hands clenched into two, white fists. "Chels—" Lisha began, reaching for her friend.

Chelsea shook her off. "Don't talk about him like . . . like he's a piece of meat or something." she seethed.

"Why not?" Bigfoot tossed out wickedly.

"Because he's a special person!" Chelsea cried. "He and I . . . he and I . . ."

"He and you what?" Bigfoot goaded. "You think Nick is *yours*?"

"Yes," Chelsea said. "Nick doesn't care about Jazz. He never did!"

Everyone in the room seemed to gasp. Lisha put her hands over her face.

Roxanne laughed ostentatiously. "Oh, come on, Chelsea. Do you really expect us to believe that he'd choose you over Jazz? Why? Because your daddy killed a bunch of innocent people and you got famous for about five minutes because of it? You are really pathetic."

Tears sprang to Chelsea's eyes.

Lisha felt terrible. *I wish I could stop Chelsea from taking Bigfoot's bait,* she thought. *I know she's playing Chelsea, I just don't know why.*

Chelsea walked around the conference table and stared hard at Roxanne. "You despicable—"

Roxanne stood up. She reached for Chelsea's arm. "Don't tell me you're in love with Nick Shaw!" she asked, feigning shock.

"I *am* in love with him," Chelsea said proudly. "I don't care who knows it."

Roxanne laughed gleefully. "Well, now the whole world knows it. Smile, honey, you're on a hidden camera!"

Everyone in the room gasped as Roxanne whirled around and removed the front from what had looked to be an ordinary television set, to reveal a hidden camera. Everyone began talking at once.

Chelsea backed away from Roxanne, her face horrified. Lisha quickly came over to her friend and led her back to the other side of the room. Everyone was talking loudly at once, pointing to the camera, and checking out Chelsea to see how she was going to react to what had just occurred.

"I'm going to kill her," Chelsea told Lisha, her back to the others in the room.

"Chill out," Lisha told her. "Now is not the time to—"

"She is a loathsome human being," Chelsea said.

"I know," Lisha agreed. "But right now you need to take a deep breath and see where this is heading."

Chelsea took a deep breath.

"Good," Lisha said. "Now, turn around and face her."

Chelsea turned around. From the other side of the room, Bigfoot's face mocked her. "The footage we just shot will be used for a show next week called 'Lovers and Losers.' It was my idea to set up this little home video. But I think Jazz is really brave to agree to have her own life be part of the show, don't you?"

A few of the employees applauded. Some others had the grace to look embarrassed or disgusted.

"You can't use that on the air without Chelsea's permission," Lisha called out.

"Please," Roxanne snorted, gathering up her papers. "Okay, our little love fest is over. Everyone, back to the trenches! One last thing. No one tells Nick Shaw about this. Or they will no longer be employed here."

"Come with me," Lisha said, practically dragging Chelsea across the conference room until they stood in front of Sumtimes. "Did you know what she was doing?" she demanded of their only friend among the executive staff.

"No," Sumtimes said. "I didn't."

"So, you have to stop her, then," Lisha said.

"I can't," Sumtimes confessed, fiddling with one of the dozen earrings in her left ear.

"What do you mean, 'you can't'?" Lisha demanded. "She's not your boss!"

"And I'm not her boss," Sumtimes pointed out.

"Bye-bye!" Roxanne sang out as she limped out of the conference room. "I'm sure you'll look lovely on camera as always, *Chutney!*"

Lisha wanted to reach out and strangle Roxanne. Chelsea had tears in her eyes, but they were blazing with anger. "I can't take this anymore. I really can't!"

Sumtimes looked around to make sure everyone had filed out of the conference room, then she put her hand on Chelsea's shaking arm. "You two never heard what I'm about to tell you, okay?"

Chelsea and Lisha nodded. "Roxanne got a letter in the mail, telling her that someone has been secretly videotaping behind the scenes at *Trash*."

Lisha hoped her face didn't betray the panic she felt. She and her friends had been making a secret, underground video that would expose the truth about how trashy *Trash* really was. Lately they had stopped, because they had come so close to getting caught.

Evidently someone had outed them to Roxanne.

"Did the letter say who was doing it?" Lisha asked carefully.

"I don't know," Sumtimes said. "But that's where Roxanne got the idea for this little stunt. I told her that if anyone actually was secretly videotaping here, I was pretty sure it was illegal. And I'm pretty sure it would be illegal for her to show the video she just made without your permission."

"Are you sure?" Chelsea asked.

"No," Sumtimes admitted. "I'm not a lawyer. But if I were you, I'd talk to one. Unless you don't mind if Jazz runs the video—"

"I mind," Chelsea said flatly.

"I thought so," Sumtimes agreed. She sighed. "I'd be really bummed if someone was making secret videos around here. It would be so totally disloyal, you know?"

Lisha managed to nod at Sumtimes.

"Just remember, you never heard any of this from me," Sumtimes reminded them. "Hey, what do you think of Paris?"

Lisha was confused. "It's a great city."

"No, as a name. I'm trying out Paris Sumtimes this week. I like the ring of it. Well, gotta get. And you guys do, too." Sumtimes hustled out of the conference room.

Chelsea shook her head and fell heavily into one of the large, leather chairs. "Do you think—"

"I don't think anything!" Lisha said loudly, pulling Chelsea up. "Come with me."

"Where?"

"Come on!" Lisha half dragged Chelsea down the hall to the nearest ladies' room. Then, when she was sure no one was inside but them, she turned on the water in all the sinks, and pushed Chelsea and herself into the same stall.

"Would you mind telling me what's going on?" Chelsea asked.

"I was afraid you'd say something about our video in the conference room," Lisha explained. "The room could still be bugged."

"Oh, right," Chelsea said. Her arm was crammed into Lisha's shoulder. "Does that also explain why we're both in this stall right now?"

"The ladies' room could be bugged, too," Lisha said.

"Ah," Chelsea acknowledged. "And the running water?"

"So no one can hear us," Lisha explained.

"You know you're crazy, don't you?" Chelsea said. "Let's get out of this stall."

Lisha got out first. Chelsea followed.

"Okay, maybe I went a little overboard," Lisha admitted, pacing across the bathroom. "But the running water stays on. Now, who sent Roxanne that note?"

"It could be Winston," Chelsea guessed. "He knows about us. And he was only keeping his mouth shut to try and get next to you."

"I'll try to find out," Lisha said. "Meanwhile I say we go call Karma."

"I don't want to tell her about the letter Roxanne got," Chelsea said quickly. "She'll worry. And she doesn't need stress right now."

"Agreed," Lisha replied. "But we'll tell her about the stunt Roxanne just pulled. Karma knows as much as any lawyer. And if she doesn't know the law, she'll find out!"

"Well, basically," Karma whined into the phone that evening, "what I found out is that you are screwed."

"That can't be true," Chelsea protested through her phone in her bedroom of their apartment. Lisha was on the cordless in the living room.

Lisha and Chelsea had called Karma from work that afternoon and told her about the

95

stunt Bigfoot had pulled. Karma had promised she'd find out what they needed to know and get back to them.

"It is," Karma said. "Evidently the law is different from state to state. But the deal is that anything you say or do at work becomes fair game for your employer. It's kind of like all those people who secretly videotaped their nannies abusing their kids."

"But I didn't abuse anyone," Chelsea cried into the phone.

"Too true," Karma agreed. "Bigfoot is the abuser, and you are the abused. However, the law is the law."

"Well, then, the law is stupid!" Chelsea yelled.

"Don't yell at the messenger, Chels," Lisha said.

"I just can't believe it." Chelsea was fuming. "You're telling me I have no recourse? I can either smile and let her run that video on national TV or I can quit?"

"You quit, and she'll still run it on national TV," Karma said. "In fact, she'll say you quit because you lost Nick to Jazz. You know I loathe and detest her, but it is diabolically wonderful, in its own sick way."

"That's what you always say about her," Chelsea said.

"I know," Karma admitted. "She's lethal, but she fascinates me."

"I think what we have to do," Lisha said

slowly, "is we have to tell Nick, no matter what Bigfoot decreed."

So far Lisha and Chelsea hadn't said a word to him. Evidently none of the other female staff from *Trash* had told him, either, although he had come up to Lisha in the afternoon and said it seemed like all the women at work were staring at him and whispering.

"Nick will get Jazz to stop this," Chelsea said firmly.

"You don't believe that," Lisha said.

"You're right." Chelsea sighed. "She wants the controversy. She lives for the publicity. All he could do is quit, which wouldn't help his life any. Do you realize the trashy newspapers are going to be all over us when this comes out? I can just see the headline: 'Burger Barn Shooter's Daughter in Lust with *Trash* Host's Boy-Toy.' "

"We owe it to Nick to tell him the truth," Lisha insisted. "He can make his own decision about what he wants to do. And if Bigfoot fires us for telling him, too bad."

"Is this the Lisha I know and love talking?" Karma asked, teasing. "The one who thinks we should do anything at all to keep our jobs at *Trash* so we can work in our chosen field?"

"Right now our chosen field is making me want to hurl," Lisha said. "Let's invite the guys over here and tell all of them."

"You're willing to be in the same room with Sky and Alan?" Chelsea asked.

"Why, what happened?" Karma demanded. "Did I miss good dirt?"

"Great dirt," Lisha admitted. She quickly told Karma what had happened with her and Sky and Alan.

"Wow"—Karma marveled—"I almost die during surgery and everything changes, huh?"

"When are you coming home?" Chelsea asked.

"Thursday, if everything goes okay," Karma said. "I can't wait to get out of here. They haven't even let me wash my hair. I mean, talk about heartless."

"Your party is going to be sensational," Chelsea promised.

"There's just one thing," Karma said slowly. "My parents really want me to come home to recuperate."

"But you can't." Lisha protested. "I mean, this is your home."

"Believe me, Long Island is not my idea of a good time," Karma whined. "My mother considers stir-fried tofu a culinary feast. She serves herbal tea instead of coffee. I will probably die there."

"Will it do any good for us to talk to her?" Chelsea asked.

"You can try," Karma said. "But for old peace-and-love hippies, my parents can be very stubborn."

"We'll work on them," Lisha promised. "We'll see you tomorrow after work."

"Bring junk food," Karma instructed. "I would kill for an extra-large Hershey bar with almonds."

Lisha picked nervously at a cuticle while she waited for Sky to join them in their living room. It was two hours later, and Nick, Alan, Chelsea, and she had just finished off two large pizzas. Sky had told Nick he'd be home around nine, and Lisha and Chelsea really didn't want to tell the guys what had happened that day without all of them being together.

Chelsea looked at her watch. "It's after nine."

"What's the biggie?" Nick asked, feeding a small piece of pepperoni to Belch.

"Don't give him that, you know it makes him barf!" Lisha exclaimed.

"Belch never barfs," Nick said with dignity.

"Tell that to our rug," Lisha retorted, eyeing the stain near the couch from their last pizza party, during which Belch had upchucked his share of the pepperoni.

"Are we waiting for Sky for some special reason?" Alan asked sharply.

His voice sounds so cold, Lisha thought. *It's my fault, too. He's hurt. And I'm the one who hurt him.*

"I told you," Chelsea said. "There's something important we need to talk about. All of us."

Alan got up. "Well, I've got two hours to put in on my novel tonight, so if you don't mind—"

There was a knock on the door. The guys had left a note in their apartment for Sky to come across the hall, so Lisha knew who was knocking. She opened the door.

"Hi," he said, smiling at her and leaning against the door frame. "What's up?"

Lisha tried not to feel flustered just looking at him. She smiled back.

God, he's so gorgeous, she thought.

"Hi," Lisha said, smiling back. "We're having a group meeting to discuss some stuff that's come up at work."

"Uh, could I join you guys later?" Sky asked. "I'm kind of . . . busy now."

"Not really," Lisha said. "This is really serious. I made everyone else wait for—"

"Sky!" a female voice called from the elevator banks. The voice's owner rounded the corner.

It was Fawn.

"There you are," she cooed, hurrying over to him. She put her arm through his and leaned her head against his chest. "Oh, hi, Lisha," she added, her voice flat.

"Now I see why you're busy," Lisha said coldly. "I wouldn't want to keep you from your *date.*"

"It's not just a date," Fawn cried happily, her eyes shining. "It's much more special than that. You see, Sky and I are engaged."

"**F**awn, we're not engaged," Sky said, chagrined. He tried to pull away from her, but she held on tight.

"Okay then," Fawn corrected, nuzzling into his chest, "we're engaged to be engaged. How's that?"

"I'm so happy for you both," Lisha told them, her voice flat. "I hope you and your child bride will be really happy together." She started to close the door in Sky's face.

"Wait! Lish!" Sky put his foot into the door to prevent her from closing it.

"Come on, Sky," Fawn said, pulling on his arm, "let's go over to your apartment, and—"

Sky shook Fawn off. "I left the door open," he told her. "Go back over there and wait for me."

"But—"

"Fawn," he warned her.

She sighed ostentatiously. "Oh, okay. But hurry up." She turned and flounced into the guys' apartment.

"This is not what it looks like," Sky told Lisha, his voice low.

"It doesn't have anything to do with me," Lisha said, giving her patented, cool shrug. "Are you coming in or not?"

Sky walked into the apartment.

Lisha shut the door and followed him. She avoided everyone's eyes in the room.

I wonder if everyone heard all of that, she thought. *How utterly humiliating. What did Fawn mean? Are she and Sky really together? Why, why, why did I let him into my heart?*

"So," Chelsea said, her voice a little too loud. "Let's talk."

They did hear, Lisha realized. She looked over at Alan out of the corner of her eye. He looked disgusted.

"About what?" Nick asked. "Sky's engagement?"

"Oh man," Sky groaned, "can't you all just pretend you never heard that?"

"Sure we can," Lisha said, her voice hard. "Because none of us *cares.*"

"I care," Alan said. "How interesting. Just how many girls are you involved with at once, Sky?"

"That's so not funny," Sky shot back.

"I didn't mean it to be," Alan said.

"Stop it," Lisha demanded. "I mean it."

Alan and Sky scowled at each other. Lisha felt guilt wash over her.

Sky and Alan are roommates. And best friends, she thought miserably. *This would be like Chelsea or Karma taking away the guy I loved.*

And to think all this time Sky has been fooling around with the fifteen-year-old.

She forced herself to concentrate on her reason for calling the meeting, to put all thoughts of her personal life aside for the moment. "Let's talk about what happened at work today."

"What happened?" Nick asked, scratching Belch behind his ears. Belch panted with happiness.

Lisha proceeded to relate to the guys that morning's meeting with Bigfoot.

Nick stopped scratching Belch about midway through the story. His face grew pale. "I don't believe it."

"Believe it," Chelsea snapped. "And it's going to be on national TV next week. The question is, what are we going to do about it?"

Belch rolled over on to his back, clearly hoping that Nick would rub his stomach. "I don't see that we have a lot of options," Nick said slowly.

"*We* can't do much," Lisha said. "*You* need to confront Jazz about this."

"I totally agree," Sky said. "When someone is playing you like that, you can't let them get away with it."

"Kind of like how Fawn is playing you?" Lisha asked, her voice biting.

"We'll talk about that later," Sky said quietly.

"No need," Lisha assured him breezily.

"Lish—"

"I'm not interested," Lisha insisted.

Sky shook his head disgustedly.

"I'll confront Jazz," Nick said. "That's not the problem. The problem is that it isn't going to do any good."

"True," Alan agreed from where he sat on the rug, his back propped up against the couch. "The only thing that would change the situation is if you gave up Chelsea and told Jazz you wanted her back."

"This whole thing is about jealousy," Lisha agreed. "Jazz just can't accept the fact that she lost you to Chelsea."

"I'm not some kind of prize in a box of Cracker Jacks, you know," Nick said. "Man, I hate this crap! I feel like an idiot. My private life is private, and—"

"Like you didn't know when you started dating Jazz that it wouldn't be private," Lisha scoffed. "Come on!"

"Hey, I met her in a club, remember? I didn't go looking to get next to someone famous."

"But you didn't exactly run away from it when she wanted to get next to you, either," Lisha pointed out.

"Jazz is gorgeous," Sky said.

"So?" Lisha snapped.

"Y'all, please, this isn't getting us anywhere," Chelsea said, her Southern drawl becoming more apparent as it always did when she was tired and stressed. "Lisha and I didn't even tell y'all everything yet. There's more bad news."

Lisha nodded. "The reason that Bigfoot even came up with the idea for this little hidden video stunt is because someone sent her a letter and outed our underground video to her!"

Sky swore under his breath.

"We're dead," Alan muttered.

"Not yet," Chelsea said. "Sumtimes is the one who told us—in total confidence. Evidently Bigfoot doesn't know who's been making the secret video."

"It won't take long for her start to suspect us," Alan said.

"I can kiss getting into the union good-bye now," Sky moaned.

"Not so fast," Chelsea said.

"Right." Lisha looked at her friends. "Right now it's no more than someone's say-so. There is no proof. Bigfoot can't do anything without proof. And we haven't had the Trash-cam at work for a long time now."

Nick stood up, and Belch began to jump around at his feet. "I'm going to call Jazz."

"Now?" Chelsea asked.

"Now," Nick said. "I don't need to work at *Trash* that much. I don't even care about a gig in TV-land. I know you guys do. But I'm not going to stand by and watch her pull this stupid stunt."

Chelsea went over to him. "What do you think she'll say?"

"I don't know," Nick admitted, looping some hair behind his ear. "I guess I'm about to find out." He smiled at Chelsea, who moved into his arms.

"You're terrific," she told him.

He hugged her close. "Let's go for a walk first, huh?" he asked her.

She nodded. The two of them walked out of the apartment, hand in hand.

Alan got up, too. "We need to get together again after Nick talks to Jazz. I'll see y'all." He hurried out of the apartment, deliberately not looking at Lisha or Sky.

Well, I guess I can't blame him, Lisha thought. *Why would he even want to be around me after what I did to him?*

Over Sky.

Sky. Who's engaged to a fifteen-year-old millionaire.

Everyone had left. She and Sky were alone. She busied herself cleaning up the empty pizza boxes.

"Lish?" Sky stood in front of her.

She moved around him and threw the boxes into the trash. "What?"

He followed her into the kitchen. "About what Fawn said—"

"It's none of my business," Lisha said.

"Come on, Lish, that's stupid—"

"Don't call me stupid," she snapped. "Go hang out with your little friend. She's waiting for you."

He threw his hands into the air. "Why are you being like this?"

"Like what?"

"Like there's nothing between us!"

"Why?" Lisha asked. "Because I know the truth!"

"The truth about *what*?" Sky asked.

"About you and Fawn."

"Lisha, you must be kidding. Fawn and I are not—"

"Let me ask you a question, then," Lisha interrupted. She turned to face him. "Is it true that if you marry Fawn, you get five million dollars from her father?"

Silence.

Then finally: "Yeah. It's true."

"I knew it," Lisha said bitterly. "No wonder you're dating her. Do you have to wait until she's eighteen to marry her, or is her daddy in so much of a hurry to land you in the family that he—"

"Lish, stop it." Sky said, taking her by the shoulders. "It isn't like that."

"So explain it to me, then," Lisha demanded, folding her arms.

Sky walked away from her, and looked out the window.

"Look, it's true that Fawn's father . . . he really cares about me. And it's true that he's rich. And it's true that nothing would make him happier than to see me marry Fawn."

"I already knew all of that," Lisha said, her voice cold. "Not because you had the guts to tell me, of course. Fawn told Alan. Alan told me."

Sky turned back to her. "But, Lish, I'm not dating the kid. That is all in her imagination."

"So what's she doing with you, then?"

"Her parents have been fighting a lot lately," Sky said. "I've been hanging out with her to help her get through it. That's all it is. I swear it!"

"Her parents let their fifteen-year-old daughter come over to an eighteen-year-old guy's apartment? Are they on drugs?"

Sky laughed. "Since when did you get so conservative?"

"That isn't conservative, that's brains," Lisha replied. "I can see what their daughter is up to, even if they can't."

"Oh, come on—"

"No, Sky. I mean it. In fact, I bet her parents know exactly how she feels about you. I bet they're just hoping you get her pregnant so that you have to get married—"

"That's ridiculous—"

"It is not," Lisha maintained. "I really do get it now. Her parents are pretending they don't know what's going on, but they're really manipulating the whole thing!"

"You don't even know Fawn's parents," Sky said, his voice angry.

"I don't need to know them," Lisha flung back. "And you're blinded by their millions."

"That is totally unfair," Sky said. "I don't care about their money."

"You are so full of it!" Lisha stormed across the room. Anything to get away from the heat she felt just being near him. She whirled on him. "If you don't care about their money, why did you take me all the way to their restaurant in Connecticut in their private plane, answer me that?"

Sky scowled at her silently.

"You wanted to impress me," Lisha went on. "So you have rich friends. So they treat you like a son. You love it. You just don't want to admit that it comes with strings called Fawn!"

From opposite ends of the room, Lisha and Sky stared at one another. Neither spoke.

Finally, Lisha walked over to him. "You're stupid," she said softly.

"Thanks a lot."

"I mean it. If you're telling me the truth, then you're really stupid. You might think you're only hanging out with Fawn, but she's in love with you. Can't you see that?"

"She is not—"

"She is," Lisha insisted. "And you love the idea of getting all that money. Even if it means marrying Fawn one day."

"I am so far away from even thinking about marriage in my life," Sky said. "I have no reason to think about it."

"I can think of five million great reasons," Lisha said bluntly. "Have you ever kissed Fawn?"

"I thought you didn't care," Sky said.

"I don't." She ran her fingers through her short hair. "I'm asking as a matter of curiosity."

"I've kissed her like a brother," Sky said.

"That's all?" she asked.

"Yeah, Lish, that's all," he said. "I . . . I've never felt about a girl the way that I feel about you. You want to pretend it's just this sex thing between us. But that isn't true. You know it isn't."

"A sex thing?" Lisha asked, her voice low.

"Well, it is," he admitted, staring at her mouth. "But it's more than that."

"And you really never even kissed Fawn?"

He took a step toward her.

"You never kissed her the way you kissed me the other night?" she pressed, her eyes meeting his.

Sky took another step toward her. "You mean like this?" He bent his head, and his lips softly brushed hers. His hand was on the small of her back. Gently, he brought her to him. "Or like this," he whispered, and kissed her again.

"Sky, I—"

"Shhh," he whispered, pulling her even closer. "Just kiss me, Lisha."

She did. She wrapped her arms around his neck and gave herself up to the sizzling magic

110

of his kisses, until she felt dizzy and her knees felt as if they would give out from under her.

At that moment Sky scooped her up in his arms and carried her into her bedroom. Gently, he laid her down on the bed. He sat down next to her.

"Close the door," Lisha said, her voice low.

He did.

"Lisha," he whispered, taking her into his arms.

She was lost in his kiss, when someone knocked insistently on the door.

"Sky? Are you in there?"

It was Fawn.

Sky groaned. "I forgot all about her."

"Me, too," Lisha said. "How did she even get in here?"

"Someone forgot to lock your front door!" Fawn called in, as if she had heard Lisha's question.

Lisha sat up. "I can't stand her, but we shouldn't be in here like this with her out there," she said reluctantly.

"You're right," Sky agreed. "I never should have left her alone for so long."

"I hope you're not in there having sex with the man I'm going to marry!" Fawn yelled.

"We're playing Scrabble!" Lisha yelled back nastily.

"That isn't funny! I'm coming in on the count of ten. One, two, three—"

"God, she is obnoxious," Lisha said.

"She's just a kid," Sky said. "I have to go." He gave her another quick kiss. "Can we do something together tomorrow night?"

"Yeah," Lisha agreed, smiling at him.

"Eight, nine—" Fawn yelled.

Sky strode over to the door and pulled it open. "Fawn, cut it out."

"Ten," she said with a smirk, smiling at him. "What were you doing in there?"

He took Fawn by the shoulder and turned her around. "Let's go."

Fawn looked back at Lisha over her shoulder. "I won't be fifteen forever, you know."

"Thanks for the warning," Lisha said. As Sky and Fawn left Lisha threw herself down on the bed and pulled the pillow over her head. She lay there, thinking about Sky's kisses.

I've never felt about a girl the way that I feel about you, he had said.

Did he mean it? Was it possible? And even if he did, once she gave him her heart, would she end up losing her soul, the way she had with Harley?

"Maybe not," Lisha whispered out loud. "Maybe it doesn't have to be that way."

Maybe, just maybe, she really could open her heart again. Sky wasn't Harley. And she wasn't the insecure child she had been when she did all the stupid things she had done with Harley.

Maybe this time she could fall in love, and for the first time in her life she could do it right.

9

Lisha was in the desert, and she couldn't find any water. She was crawling on her hands and knees, so thirsty, her throat so parched.

Up ahead, could it be . . . yes! Water! A beautiful pool of cool, blue water. Some people were standing in front of it. She tried to call out to them, but her throat was so dry that they couldn't hear her. She would have to crawl.

Inch by agonizing inch, she came closer to the people and the water. Could she make it? Did she have the strength? Just as she was about to lower her head to the cool, clear liquid, the people turned around.

"You can't have any water!" It was Fawn. She kicked Lisha away from the water carelessly with the edge of her expensive, designer shoes.

"Oh, we could give her a sip," the guy standing next to her said. It was Sky. He had his arm around Fawn.

"Forget it," the other guy said. His voice was evil. Lisha couldn't see his face. "She belongs with me, someplace where there *is* no water. In hell!"

The guy turned around to face Lisha. Half of his face was an ugly mask of blood and oozing puss.

The other half was Harley.

Lisha screamed. She shot up in bed, her face covered in sweat, her eyes wide open.

That was the most terrible nightmare I've ever had, she realized, gasping for breath. She looked at the clock by her bed. She had to get up for work in a half hour.

Dimly, she realized that the reason she had been dreaming about water was that her throat was killing her. She coughed. It felt as if someone were rubbing sandpaper against the inside of her throat.

She got up and padded into the bathroom, where, painful as it was to swallow, she downed two glasses of water. Then she crawled back into bed.

Great, Lisha thought, pulling the covers over her head. The water bed rocked gently as her weight settled. *Just when I thought I was finally over this thing, I'm sicker than ever.* Every part of her body hurt. She huddled back under the covers and quickly fell back asleep.

114

When Chelsea came in later to see if she was awake for work, Lisha croaked that she was sick. Chelsea said she'd call in for her. After that, Lisha fell back into a deep, dreamless sleep.

She was awakened many hours later by the insistent ringing of the telephone. "Go away," she mumbled through her sore throat. "Whatever you're selling is something I don't want."

The phone stopped ringing. She fell asleep again. The next time she opened her eyes to look at the clock, it was two o'clock in the afternoon.

She struggled to sit up. Her head was pounding. The phone rang and she answered it.

"Yeah?" she croaked through her painful throat.

"Lish? It's me," came Chelsea's voice. "I wanted to see how you were feeling. I called you before, but no one answered."

"Oh, yeah, I vaguely remember that," Lisha said. "I just woke up."

"Do you have a fever?"

Lisha felt her head. "I don't think so. But my throat really hurts and I'm totally exhausted."

"You should go see a doctor," Chelsea urged.

"I'm okay. I'll make myself some tea or something."

"Hold on a sec," Chelsea said. "Sky wants to talk to you."

"Hi," Sky said.

"Hi. I hope I didn't give you my germs last night."

"How are you feeling?"

"Not so hot," Lisha admitted.

"You want me to bring you anything on my way home after work?"

"Ice cream?" Lisha asked. "I hear when you're sick, the calories don't count."

"Rocky Road, your favorite," Sky promised.

Lisha was touched. "How did you know that?"

"I paid attention," Sky said. "See you in a few hours."

Lisha smiled as she hung up the phone. When she closed her eyes, she could picture everything that had happened the night before, she could feel Sky's kisses, his arms around her, his—

Ri-i-i-i-ng! The phone rang again.

She picked it up. "Hello?"

"May I speak with Alicia Bishop, please?" a formal-sounding female voice said.

"Speaking," Alicia said through her sore throat.

"Miss Bishop, this is Dr. de Souza, from the New York City Department of Health. I'd like to arrange for you to come in and see me."

"See you about what?" Lisha asked, confused.

"I don't want to discuss this over the phone, Miss Bishop," the doctor said. "But it's impor-

116

tant that I see you as soon as possible. Could you come this afternoon?"

"The only reason that you reached me is that I'm home from work sick," Lisha explained. "I'd really like to know what this is about."

"As I said, I'd rather speak with you in person," Dr. de Souza said. She quickly gave Lisha directions, and they agreed that Lisha would come in the next morning, unless she was running a fever.

Lisha hung up and stared at the address she had written on the scrap of paper. Why would some doctor she had never heard of at the city health department want to talk to her? Urgently?

Lisha had no idea. But just the same, she had a terrible, terrible feeling of dread.

"Thank you for coming so promptly, Miss Bishop," Dr. de Souza said, taking a seat behind her desk. She was a young woman who seemed to be doing her best to look older. She wore her flyaway dark hair in a severe bun, and the clothes under her white lab jacket were conservative and dowdy.

It was early the next morning, and Chelsea had agreed to accompany Lisha to the doctor's office before they went to work. Now they sat opposite the doctor in her tiny office, on scarred, ancient wooden chairs.

"You can call me Lisha," Lisha said. "Listen, I've been very nervous ever since you called me yesterday. What is this all about?"

Dr. de Souza made a tent with her fingers. "This is never an easy thing to do," she began hesitantly. Then she sighed and appeared to stiffen her resolve. "Miss Bishop, it is my job to inform you that you have been traced as having possibly been exposed to the HIV virus."

Chelsea gasped and reached for Lisha's hand.

Lisha's mouth dropped open. "I . . . *what?*"

Dr. de Souza repeated what she had just said.

Lisha shook off Chelsea's hand. "Wait a minute. This is a joke, right?"

"I'm afraid not," the doctor said.

"Well, then, it's a mistake," Lisha said. "I have not been exposed to AIDS." She turned to Chelsea. "It's got to be Bigfoot! This is her idea of humor!" Lisha jumped up. "I'll bet she's got a hidden camera in here, too." She whirled around, looking for a camera.

"Miss Bishop—"

Lisha turned back to the doctor. "How much did Roxanne pay you to pull off this little stunt, doctor? Hey, I'll bet you're not even really a doctor, because a real doctor would never—"

"Miss Bishop. Lisha. Please. Sit down."

Lisha sat.

"This is not a prank. I have no idea who Roxanne is," the doctor said.

Lisha just stared at her.

Dr. de Souza looked down at her papers. "I'm sorry, but according to my—"

"Maybe it wasn't Roxanne," Lisha interrupted. "But someone is trying to play a trick on me, and it isn't very funny. Who gave you my name?"

"I'm not at liberty to divulge that information," Dr. de Souza said primly.

"Oh, you're not," Lisha jeered. "Well, how ducky."

"Lisha," Chelsea began, "don't blame her—"

"What, I'm just supposed to sit here and listen to this?" Lisha asked, her voice rising.

"I know this is shocking news for you," the doctor said, smoothing a few loose strands of hair back into her bun. "But it is my job to inform you that you will need to be tested for HIV immediately. If that test is negative, depending on when your last sexual contact was, you may need to have another test in—"

"Time out, time out," Lisha interrupted again. "You don't seem to understand. I have only ever slept with *one* guy in my *entire life*."

The doctor was silent for a moment. "Well, then, I guess that narrows down the list of men who could have reported your exposure."

Lisha laughed bitterly. "I don't think so. You see, he's dead."

Dr. de Souza faltered for a moment. "Did he die from AIDS?"

"No," Lisha said. "He died when he jumped off a bridge."

The doctor opened a file on her desk and quickly read a paper inside. "I believe you were reported by a partner of your partner," she explained.

Lisha's heart began to pound. Sweat beaded on her forehead. "Are you telling me . . . are you telling me that Harley slept with someone, and that someone is HIV positive, and she knew she got it from him, and she knew about me, and named me?"

The doctor hesitated again. "I'm sorry, I'm not allowed—"

Lisha jumped up and clutched the edge of the doctor's desk, her knuckles white. "Please. You can't just sit there and not help me. Harley was a drug addict. He could have died with the HIV virus and never even have known he had it. I have to know—"

The young doctor stared back at Lisha, her face compassionate and concerned. "I . . . all I can tell you is that . . . your assumptions may be correct," she said gently.

Lisha fell back into the chair.

"Lish?" Chelsea reached for Lisha's hand.

"I . . . I . . ." Lisha couldn't speak. The room was spinning.

This has to be a nightmare, she thought wildly. *I'm probably running a fever. That must be it. I'm having an even worse nightmare than the one about Fawn and Sky and Harley.*

This can't be real. I'm going to wake up. This isn't really happening to me.

Lisha shut her eyes tight, but when she opened them, it was all too true. The doctor. The clinic.

Exposure to AIDS.

And a sore throat I can't get rid of, she thought, panicking. *No energy.*

Oh, God . . .

Lisha lurched out of her chair, holding her stomach. "I'm going to be—"

"Through there," the doctor said, pointing to a door to the right.

Lisha ran into the bathroom. She sank to her knees in front of the toilet and vomited again and again, until there was nothing left inside of her. It was a long time before she dimly realized that Chelsea was with her, stroking her hair.

"Oh, God, Chels," Lisha whispered.

"It doesn't mean you have AIDS," Chelsea said.

"But I might," Lisha said, tears coming to her eyes. "You shouldn't be touching me—"

"Look, even if you do have it, I can't get it by touching you," Chelsea said.

The doctor knocked politely on the open door of the bathroom. "I brought you a cup of cold water," she said, handing a paper cup to Chelsea, who handed it to Lisha.

"Thank you," Lisha managed. She drank down the water, her hands shaking. Then she looked up at Dr. de Souza. "What do I do now?"

"We do a blood test. You'll have the results in three days."

"Three days," Lisha repeated shakily. She got up. "All right. Do we do it now?"

"Yes," Dr. de Souza said. "I can do the test now. Just step next door with me into the lab room."

Lisha went into the lab room and sat in a chair with a tray that swung in front of her.

"Put your arm on that to steady it, please," the doctor instructed as she donned a pair of rubber gloves. Then she took a piece of rubber tubing and tied it above Lisha's elbow. She dabbed a spot with alcohol, inserted the needle, and Lisha watched her blood flowing into the tiny vial.

My blood that might be poisoned, she thought dully. *I could die. No, that can't be true. Yes, it could.*

"I have a pamphlet to give you that you need to read thoroughly," the doctor said briskly, removing her gloves and throwing them away. "It will explain everything you need to do or not do while you're waiting for the results of your test."

"I have two roommates," Lisha said, gulping hard. She shoved the pamphlet into her pocket. "Do I move out?"

"No need to do that," Dr. de Souza replied.

"Although you might want to inform them that you're waiting for these test results. It's only fair. You might be a little agitated."

Lisha nodded. "Do I have to tell my employer?"

"No," the doctor said. "You don't have to do anything except be scrupulous about not sharing your body fluids with anyone. And remember, Lisha, your test may very well be negative—"

"Dr. de Souza?" a plump, young African-American technician asked from the doorway, her voice startled. "Why are you taking blood? I mean, you're a doctor. That's my job!"

"I just thought I'd help out," the doctor said kindly. "Miss Bishop was a little nervous."

"Well, I don't know, doctor," the technician objected. "I know you're new here and everything, but you're still the doctor. Doctors don't draw blood."

"This doctor just did," Dr. de Souza said firmly.

The technician frowned, turned on her heel, and walked away.

Lisha got up and ran her fingers through her hair, which was damp with perspiration. "So, what, I call you, or something?"

"No, we'll call you when your test results are in," Dr. de Souza said. "And then you'll come in and see me."

"I guess you don't like to tell people over the phone, huh, doctor?" Lisha asked, trying to

123

cover her terror by being tough. "I mean, think of all the messy suicides that could occur—"

Dr. de Souza reached into her pocket and brought out a white card. "Here's my card. My home phone is on there."

Lisha just stared at the card.

"And Lisha?"

Lisha looked up at the doctor.

"My first name is Shveta. You can use it. And you can call me."

"Lisha?"

"Go away."

Lisha lay in her darkened bedroom, staring up at the ceiling. Since she and Chelsea had returned to their apartment an hour ago, she had cried so many tears that she didn't think there was any liquid left inside her body. And yet still more tears leaked out, silently, onto her damp pillow.

Chelsea ignored her friend's request and came farther into the room. She had called in sick for both of them. "Can I get you anything?"

"A new life," Lisha said.

Chelsea sat on the edge of Lisha's bed. "I really believe that the test is going to be negative, Lish."

"What if it isn't?" Lisha asked.

"Well, then we'll deal with it when we have to deal with it," Chelsea said.

"No, *we* won't deal with it," Lisha corrected. "*I'll* deal with it. I can't stay here if I'm—"

"Yes, you can," Chelsea said firmly.

Lisha sat up. "Wouldn't you be afraid?"

"It's not so easy to catch HIV, you know. Think of all the families where one family member is HIV positive. None of the other family members ever come down with it. Even wives and husbands; if they follow the rules about safe sex."

"We'll have to tell Karma," Lisha said.

"We will," Chelsea agreed. "But I know she'll feel the same way I feel."

Lisha stared at her friend. *If Chelsea were the one who might be HIV positive, would I be so wonderful about it?* she wondered. *Or would I be afraid of catching it?*

I'd be afraid, Lisha realized, feeling ashamed of herself.

"What are you going to do about Sky?" Chelsea asked.

Lisha buried her face in her hands. "I can't tell him."

"But you have to!"

"No, I don't." Lisha insisted. She stared at Chelsea, wild-eyed. "Thank God, I never slept with Alan. We were so close that night . . . and the other night I almost did it with Sky! What if I had? What if I had infected him?"

"But you didn't."

"I didn't," Lisha agreed. "But . . . but the kisses . . ."

"You can't get it from kissing," Chelsea said. "That's what I heard."

"Well, what if you heard wrong? What if I gave it to him and Alan?"

Chelsea reached out and hugged Lisha. "You didn't. I know you didn't. I don't even think you have it."

"But look how sick I've been," Lisha said, still more tears traveling down her face. "HIV compromises your immune system, right? Well, what about my cough, and my sore throat—"

"That doesn't mean anything. Lots of people get coughs and sore throats."

Lisha shook her head violently. "I can't tell anyone. Not anyone. Except you and Karma."

"Lisha—"

"I can't!" she cried wildly. "And you can't, either! Promise me you won't tell anyone!"

Chelsea sighed. "You only have to wait three days for the test results, Lish. I won't tell anyone before then."

Lisha grasped Chelsea's hand. "If it's positive, you can't tell anyone after that, either."

"Lisha—"

"Chelsea, please! You have to do this for me! You have to promise!"

"I promise," Chelsea said quietly.

"Thank you," Lisha said. Her hands were shaking. "I'm just going to have to break up with Sky."

"But, Lish, that doesn't make sense. I'm sure that in three days your test results will be negative, and—"

"I have to do this my way, Chelsea," Lisha

said. "If you're really my best friend, you'll let me do it."

"Okay," Chelsea said reluctantly. "But that doesn't mean I can't try to get you to change your mind."

Lisha's eyes grew wide. She gulped hard. "Chelsea, what if . . . what if I die?"

The room was silent. The only answer was the voices of Lisha's demons in her head.

Harley had always told her that if he couldn't have her, no one could.

Somewhere far, far away, Lisha thought she heard the sound of Harley laughing.

"Lisha, this is Sumtimes," came the voice through the phone the next day. "How are you feeling?"

Lisha sat up in bed and tried to keep her hands from shaking. *How I am feeling is terrified,* she wanted to say. *I can't eat. I can't sleep. I have terrible nightmares. I'm dying. And I can't tell anyone.*

But she didn't say any of that. Sumtimes and everyone else at work thought she had bronchitis. "I'm a little better," Lisha managed hoarsely. She coughed into the phone.

Actually, she felt quite a lot better physically. Her throat didn't hurt nearly as much, and her cough was almost gone.

But there's no way I can face life at Trash *until I know the results of my HIV test,* Lisha thought.

Hence, the bronchitis excuse.

"So, how much longer do you think you'll be out of work?" Sumtimes asked. "With you and Karma both out sick, Roxanne is on the warpath."

"Not too long," Lisha said evasively.

"Well, we all miss you," Sumtimes said. "Listen, you didn't tell anyone what I told you about Jazz and that anonymous letter she got, did you?"

"No," Lisha said. "Why?"

"For some reason Jazz has called off the 'Lovers and Losers' show, where she was planning to show the video of Chelsea admitting that she's in love with Nick."

"I'm glad to hear it," Lisha said.

"I am, too," Sumtimes agreed. "I just can't figure out why she did it. It isn't like Jazz to do anything nice for—" She caught herself. "I mean, she doesn't change her mind about a show very often. So, feel better!"

Sumtimes hung up, and so did Lisha. She looked at the clock on her nightstand. It was two o'clock in the afternoon. The apartment was deadly quiet. Chelsea was at *Trash*. Karma had been released from the hospital that morning, but her parents had refused to let her come back to the apartment. She was at their house on Long Island. Lisha hadn't told Karma yet about her HIV test. She kept putting it off.

Lisha stared up at the ceiling. *Nothing seems real,* she thought. *In two days I could get a death sentence. This is the kind of thing that is only supposed to happen to other people. Not to me. Not to me!*

Just then she heard an insistent knock on the front door of the apartment.

"Who could that be?" she wondered out loud. She got out of bed, looked down at her cutoffs and white T-shirt, and shrugged. "I don't care how I look," she told herself as she hurried to the front door.

"Who is it?" she called through the door.

"Sky," came the voice back.

Sky. Oh, God.

"I'm probably contagious," Lisha called back. "So I can't let you in."

"Get over it, Lish," he called back. "Bronchitis isn't catchy. Besides, I'm sure you already gave me any germs you might have."

I don't want to see him, I don't want to face him, she thought, feeling tears rising to her eyes.

"Come on, Lish!" he called. "I snuck away from the *Trash* heap and brought you some of your favorite stuff."

Slowly, Lisha unlocked the door. Sky bounded into the living room carrying two bags of groceries. He kissed her and headed into the kitchen to put them down. "Okay, Dr. Sky is in the house, ladies and gentlemen!" He began to lift things out of one of the grocery bags. "What have we here, you might ask? Let's see—two kinds of ice cream, hot fudge sauce, the kind of kosher hot dogs Karma usually gets for you—I know you love those—"

"Sky . . ."

"Super-chunk peanut butter—feel free to mix it into the ice cream—"

"Sky, I'm not hungry."

"Wait, there's more!" he cried, reaching into the other bag. "I got all the things Karma would have gotten for you—chicken soup with matzo balls, bagels, lox spread—"

"I mean it, Sky," Lisha said, hardening her voice. "I'm not hungry. You wasted your money."

He stopped unpacking and looked at her. "Well, maybe you'll get hungry."

She didn't reply.

"Hey, so, did you get some sleep?"

"A little."

He put his arms around her waist. "Want Dr. Sky's famous back rub before I go back to work?"

"No," Lisha forced herself to say. "I just . . . I just want to be alone."

Sky looked hurt. "I can come back later, after work—"

"Go hang out with Fawn," Lisha said.

He cocked his head to one side. "What's up with you?"

I can't tell you, she thought miserably. *I could be dying. I could poison you with my blood.*

She looked away from him so that he wouldn't

see the terror in her eyes. "Nothing's up," she said. "I'm just not ready for a relationship, Sky."

Gently he turned her face back to his. "Is that what this is about? You think I'm gonna get all heavy on you?" He laughed. "Lish, that is not my style."

"No, I mean I don't want *any* kind of relationship," she said firmly.

Sky faltered. "You mean you . . . what do you mean?"

I have to push him away, Lisha thought. *If it turns out I'm not HIV positive, I'll explain it all to him then. But if I tell him the truth now, he'll think he has to be nice to me and pretend that everything is the same when it isn't.*

She forced herself to stare him in the eye. "What I mean is that you and I . . . it's a mistake. I'm sorry."

She could see how hurt he was. "You don't really mean that, Lish—"

"I do," she said firmly.

"What is it, you're not over that crazed guy you used to be involved with . . . Harley?"

If you only knew, Lisha thought.

"It's not that," she said.

"So, what is it, then?" he asked. "Is there another guy?"

"No," Lisha said. "I just don't want a relationship right now. I don't . . . I don't think we're right for each other."

Sky pressed his lips together. He ran his hand through his hair. "It's Alan, isn't it?"

"No—"

"Believe me, Lish, I feel guilty about Alan, too. He's one of my best friends. But you can't help who you fall in love with—"

Love. Does that mean he loves me? Oh, Sky.

"It isn't Alan," she forced herself to say.

He reached out for her. His hand caressed her cheek. "I don't believe you don't want to be with me, Lish. The other night, in your bedroom, when we almost—"

She took a step back from him. "I'm telling you, Sky, it was a mistake."

"But I know you wanted to be with me as much as—"

"That's just lust." Lisha was beginning to sound desperate. "It doesn't mean anything!"

His eyes searched hers. "So . . . you have no feelings for me?"

Lisha gulped hard. "Only as a friend, Sky. I'm sorry. You should be with Fawn. She really loves you."

Sky's hands dangled at his sides. "Okay. I've never forced myself on a girl yet and I don't intend to start." His voice was hard, hurt. "I'm sorry I ever bothered you with my affection."

She wanted to reach out to him. She wanted to cry in his arms, and be comforted by the sound of his heart beating in her ear as she lay her head on his muscular chest.

But I can't, she thought. *I can't.*

"I guess I'll leave," Sky said, shoving his hands into the pockets of his jeans.

"I think you should."

After one more searching look, he turned and walked out of the apartment.

Lisha locked the door after him. Then she put her back against the door and cried until her stomach ached. Then she slid down the door into a ball on the floor, and rocked herself, and cried some more.

Lisha could hear Chelsea bustling around the kitchen, making dinner, as she sat on her bed and reread the terrible letter that she'd just received in the mail. It was from a girl named Jennie Blythstone, whom Lisha had known when she'd lived in Europe with Harley. Jennie was wild, and she had spent a year bumming around Europe, getting into as much trouble as she could. She'd had a huge crush on Harley, and she was always flirting with him. Today, Lisha had received this letter from Jennie in the mail.

Dear Lisha,

I'm probably the last person you thought you'd hear from. I can't say that I'm happy to be writing this letter to you. I got your address from your parents. If you haven't gotten this bad news yet, I'm writing to tell you that recently I found out that I'm

HIV positive. I know who gave it to me, too. It was Harley. We were fooling around behind your back when you guys were together. I'm not proud of it, but it's the truth. Then, after you left Harley, he and I got together. When I came back to the States, he came and stayed with me for a while. But then his drug thing got too intense, and we broke up. After that I got sick with hepatitis, and I wasn't with any other guys. That's how I know it had to be Harley who infected me. I'm taking a lot of medications and so far I feel fine. I try not to think about dying. Maybe they'll come up with a cure. I'm sorry I have to tell you about this, but you need to get tested if you haven't gotten tested already. I never, ever thought this could happen to me. If you want to talk or anything, you can call me.

Jennie

Lisha felt sick to her stomach.

Jennie Blythstone is the person who reported me to the health department. Jennie is HIV positive. Harley did that to her.

Harley could have done that to me, too.

"Hey, Lish, you think you can manage some soup?" Chelsea asked.

"No," Lisha said.

"What, then? I'll make you anything you want."

"Nothing."

Chelsea came into the living room. "Are you sure?"

Wordlessly, Lisha handed Chelsea the letter from Jennie. "This kind of kills the ol' appetite."

Chelsea quickly read the letter. She looked at Lisha. "That doesn't mean you're positive."

"Harley was cheating with her behind my back when he and I were together. He gave it to her. How could I not be positive?"

"Well . . . maybe . . . maybe he didn't get it until after you were with him," Chelsea pointed out. "She said in this letter that she was with him after you were."

Lisha held her stomach. "I have a terrible feeling."

Chelsea sat next to her and put her arms around her friend. "No matter what happens, Lish, I'll be here for you."

Tears fell silently from Lisha's eyes. "You don't have to say that, Chelsea. You have no idea what you could be letting yourself in for."

"It's okay," Chelsea insisted. "I know you'd do the same thing for me. You want to call Karma and tell her?"

"No," Lisha said, wiping her tears away with the back of her hand.

"You want me to tell her?" Chelsea asked gently.

Lisha nodded yes.

Chelsea picked up the phone and dialed Karma's parents' house. Karma's mother, Wendy, answered, and said that Karma was napping. "I'll call later," Chelsea promised, and hung up the phone. "Look, you really need to eat something, Lish. Just tell me what you want and I'll—"

"I can't," Lisha said, getting up from the couch. "I think . . . I need to get out of here."

Chelsea stood up, too. "Where are you going to go?"

"I don't know." Lisha grabbed a jean jacket from the front hall closet. "Just . . . out."

"You want company?" Chelsea offered.

Lisha shook her head no. "I just need to . . . walk, or something. And think."

"Just remember, Lisha, the test could be negative. You'll know soon. Don't assume the news will be bad."

"I'll try not to," Lisha said, doing her best to smile at her friend.

Lisha headed out the door and took the ancient elevator to the lobby. Just as she was exiting through the front doors of the building, a taxi stopped in front, and Sky got out.

With Fawn.

Even though it was exactly what Lisha had told him to do, it still broke her heart.

"Oh, hi!" Fawn said gaily, when she saw Lisha. "I'm on my way up to Sky's apartment for dinner."

"That's nice," Lisha said tonelessly.

Sky stared at Lisha. "You sure you're well enough to be up and out?"

"I'm fine," she said shortly.

Fawn grabbed Sky's arm. "I hope your roommates are gone," she told him lovingly. "I want to be all alone with you."

"I told you, Fawn, this isn't a date," Sky said, still looking at Lisha.

"That's what you think," Fawn replied with a grin.

"Could you just go into the lobby for a minute?" he asked her. "I want to talk to Lisha."

"About what?"

"If I wanted you to know, I wouldn't have asked you to go into the lobby, now, would I?" Sky asked her with exasperation.

"Fine," she said irritably, and marched into the lobby.

"I was just going for a walk," Lisha said lamely.

"You don't look too good," Sky said.

"I'm okay." She brushed her bangs off her forehead. "You should go be with Fawn."

Sky reached out for her arm. "Why?"

She couldn't speak.

"Why, Lish? I just don't get it!"

"Because she loves you," Lisha said, trying to sound flippant. "Because with her you get five million dollars. How many more reasons do you need?"

"She's not with me on a date, Lisha," Sky said. "You heard me tell her that. Her mom just went to Reno to get a quickie divorce. Her father has his girlfriend over at the mansion—"

"You don't have to explain it to me," Lisha said.

"But I want to!" Sky insisted. "Frank asked me if I could entertain Fawn tonight."

It sure didn't take Sky long to take me up on my suggestion that he be with Fawn, she thought sadly.

"Well, you can't disappoint the man who could make you a millionaire, can you?" Lisha asked. She knew she sounded nasty, but she couldn't help herself.

Sky shook his head. "I just don't get you, Lisha. First you were jealous of Fawn. Now you're throwing me at her."

"I was never jealous," Lisha maintained. "And I . . . changed my mind, that's all."

"That's not all," Sky said. "I know it's not." He took another step toward her. "I can't stop thinking about you, Lisha."

"No, Sky—"

"Your eyes look so sad. I know something is bothering you. You can't fool me. I'm not the macho jerk you seem to think I am, Lish. Please, just tell me what's really going on so I can—"

"I . . . I can't explain it to you now," Lisha murmured desperately.

"When, then?" Sky asked.

Lisha pressed her lips together to keep from crying. "Soon. Maybe. I don't know." She backed away from him.

"Lish, please . . ."

She knew she had to get away from him quickly, or she would dissolve into a puddle of tears right there on the sidewalk.

"Leave me alone, Sky!" The words were torn from her throat. "Just . . . please. If you care about me at all, leave me alone."

Then she turned away from him and ran.

But no matter how far she ran, she could still feel his eyes on her, hurt, wondering why.

L isha stared at the bad art in the living room of her apartment, but she didn't really see it. She hadn't really seen anything since that horrible moment two days earlier when Dr. de Souza had told her that she might have AIDS.

All I have to do is hang on until tomorrow, Lisha thought dully. *Tomorrow I'll find out the verdict.*

Tomorrow I'll know if I'm going to live. Or die.

It was early evening, and as befit her mood, it was pouring outside. Chelsea would be home from *Trash* soon.

Trash. It seemed so removed from her life now, from anything that was important.

The day had seemed endless. Lisha had slept until eleven o'clock, then she had tried to read a book, but she couldn't concentrate. She picked up a magazine, and there was a first-person article by a teen girl with AIDS. She wanted to read it, and she didn't want to read it, both at the same time.

The girl had lost her boyfriend.

She had lost most of her friends.

She was in and out of the hospital.

She was planning her own funeral.

That had scared Lisha so much that she'd actually picked up Dr. de Souza's home number and tried to call her, but all she got was an answering machine.

Of course, she realized. *She's at the clinic, giving more people the terrible news.*

Lisha clicked on the television, and stared at it. An advertisement for perfume came on. The girl was gorgeous. A guy chased her across the beach, because she smelled so good.

He looked a lot like Sky.

Hot tears came to Lisha's eyes, just thinking about Sky.

I hurt him, she realized. *And he doesn't know why. Just when I started to think we might really belong together, I had to push him away. But it was for his own good.*

At that moment the door opened and Chelsea walked in, shaking her umbrella, so that drops of rain scattered across the room. "Wow, it's really pouring," she said, stowing the umbrella in the overcrowded, tiny front closet. "How are you?"

"Okay."

Chelsea walked over to Lisha and sat next to her on the couch. "Did you eat anything all day?"

Lisha gave her a faint smile. "You think you have to be my Jewish mother because Karma isn't here."

"That's right," Chelsea said. "I'm worried about you."

"I'm worried about me, too," Lisha agreed grimly.

Chelsea rose and went into the kitchen to get a glass of milk. She poured one for Lisha, too, and handed it to her.

"I don't want this," Lisha said, staring at the drink.

"Drink it anyway," Chelsea urged. "You're getting too skinny."

"I heard when you have AIDS, you just, like, waste away," Lisha said.

"Well, you're wasting away from not eating," Chelsea said firmly.

"Maybe."

Chelsea sat in the overstuffed chair across from Lisha. "You'll know tomorrow, Lish. I think the not knowing is the worst thing—"

"No," Lisha said. "Knowing will be worse. At least now I can still hope."

"Why are you so convinced that you'll get bad news?"

"You read that letter from Jennie," Lisha said. "That's why."

"I really believe you're going to be negative," Chelsea said. "And even if you are positive, it isn't such a death sentence anymore, you know. I saw this special on TV where they interviewed all these people who were living with HIV, and they have all these new medicines, and—"

"Chels, I know you mean well, but this isn't helping me."

Chelsea put her empty milk glass on the coffee table. "Okay." She thought a moment. "Sky talked to me today. At lunch."

"Uh-huh."

"He told me you broke up with him."

"I did."

"But it doesn't make any sense—"

"It does to me," Lisha said stubbornly.

Chelsea's face softened. "He really cares about you, Lish."

"And I . . . I care about him, too," Lisha admitted. She felt a lump in her throat. "But it doesn't make any difference now."

Chelsea jumped up. "You are infuriating! I mean it. And when your test is negative tomorrow, you're going to have to make up with him and explain everything."

"If it's negative, I will. But if it's not, he won't have to feel like he has to pretend he wants to be with me when he'll want to run far, far away."

"How do you know?"

Because if he got AIDS, I think I'd want to

146

run away, Lisha admitted to herself. *Am I really that much worse of a person than everyone else?*

"I just do," she said.

"I think you don't give your friends enough credit, that's what I think," Chelsea said.

There was a knock on the front door. Chelsea went to answer it. "Who is it?" she asked, trying to peer through the peephole in the door.

"Trick or treat," came Karma's nasal voice.

"Karma!" Chelsea cried, hurrying to open the door. She threw her arms around her friend. "What are you doing here? How did you get here? Why didn't you use your key?"

"Let's see, white Asian sisters," Karma said, coming into the living room, "the answers to your quiz are: I live here, my mom drove me, and I didn't want to scare you. Hi, Lish."

"Hi," Lisha said halfheartedly from where she sat on the couch. She noticed that Karma looked thinner and paler, but essentially the same. She had on faded jeans with a LaCroix silver mesh T-shirt, and she wore silver lipstick to match.

"I just love your outpouring of love," Karma whined. "I missed you, too."

"I am glad to see you," Lisha said. "I'm just . . . I've got something on my mind."

"How are you feeling?" Chelsea asked Karma. "When can you come home for good?"

"I'm feeling fine, and really soon," Karma said. "I'm so crazy I even miss the Trashbin. Of course, Demetrius has been to see me just about every day, so he keeps me up on all the gossip."

"Is your mom coming up?" Chelsea asked.

Karma shook her head no and sat in the overstuffed chair. "She's going over to that new health-food restaurant on Broadway to check out the competition. There's supposed to be some new kind of burger made from soy that doesn't taste like cardboard. As if." She looked around the apartment. "I missed this place. Hey, what have you got to eat?"

"Bagels, lox spread, ice cream," Chelsea began.

Karma's jaw fell open. "How is this possible? No one shops for that stuff but me!"

"Sky brought it over for Lisha," Chelsea explained.

Karma grinned. "Oh, so you and Sky are doing a serious love-jones kind of a thing, huh?"

Lisha didn't say anything. Chelsea just looked at Lisha.

"Uh, excuse me, but did I walk into the right apartment?" Karma asked. "Did aliens steal the minds of my roomies, leaving mere human shells behind? Wow, it could be an episode of *The X-Files*."

"Lisha has something to tell you," Chelsea said slowly.

"So, tell," Karma urged.

Lisha tried, but no words would come out of

her mouth. Instead, she got up, retrieved the letter she'd gotten from Jennie Blythstone, and handed it to Karma.

Karma read the letter, then she looked up at Lisha. "Are you . . . ?"

"She doesn't know yet," Chelsea answered for Lisha. "She gets the results of the blood test tomorrow."

Wordlessly, Karma went to Lisha and put her arms around her.

"If you're nice to me, I'll lose it," Lisha said, fighting back tears.

"So, lose it," Karma said, holding on tight.

"No, I can't," Lisha said, pulling away. "I might never get it back again."

Karma nodded with understanding. "Okay, so the test is going to be negative tomorrow."

"That's what I said," Chelsea agreed. She sat on the rug near the couch.

"I know you guys mean well," Lisha said, "but those are just empty words. You don't know. And I don't know."

"You're right," Karma told her. "However, I have this incredible ESP. I might have forgotten to mention it to you. I can see into the future. What I see is that I'm making millions in the stock market this year, Chelsea is going to get the job of her dreams on *60 Minutes,* and you are going to have a negative HIV test and fall into Sky's hunky arms."

Lisha's mouth twitched with a half smile. "Oh, you think so?"

"No, I know so," Karma asserted. "I could charge for this sort of soothsaying, ya know. You're lucky I love you. For you I'm giving it away."

Lisha laughed. "You know you're crazy, don't you?"

"I do," Karma agreed. "So, what time do you get the test results?"

"We go to the health department at ten tomorrow morning," Chelsea said.

"Okay, I'm there," Karma said. "I'll tell my mom I'm spending the night."

"You don't have to—" Lisha began.

"Yeah, I have to," Karma said.

A huge lump formed in Lisha's throat again. "I don't deserve two friends like you guys."

"You know, that's true," Karma agreed. "I think I'll move out and have Janelle move in. She's what you deserve."

"Speaking of the bad seed," Lisha said, "how is your sister?"

"Out of the hospital," Karma reported. "Her parents sent me a lovely plant that you have to water, like, every two hours or something." She got up and went into the kitchen, pulling the ice cream out of the freezer. Then she got a spoon from the drawer and leaned against the counter, happily spooning ice cream into her mouth directly from the container. "You can't imagine the deprivation I've endured. Tofu ice cream."

"Horrors," Chelsea teased. "Hey, I've got an idea. How about a backwards dinner?"

"A what?" Lisha asked.

"You know, like from *Alice in Wonderland*. A backwards dinner! When I was a little girl and I was feeling really sad about something, my mom would let me have a backwards dinner. First course, all the ice cream you can eat. Second course, whatever you should have eaten for dinner in the first place."

Karma laughed. "That would be a bagel. No bagels at the hospital or at my parents' house."

"We got bagels," Lisha said, beginning to get into the spirit of things.

"So, you cut and I'll get out the cream-cheese-and-lox spread," Karma said, diving into the refrigerator, the ice-cream container still in one hand.

Chelsea got two spoons from the drawer and handed one to Lisha. They both scooped out some ice cream and ate it while they rummaged for the bagel fixings.

"So, what's this about Sky being rich?" Karma asked.

"His ex-relatives are rich," Chelsea explained. "You should see the fifteen-year-old millionairess who wants to marry him."

"I hate fifteen-year-old millionairesses on principle," Karma decreed. "And I know she's no match for Luscious Lisha."

"She thinks she is," Lisha said. "She thinks she's engaged to Sky."

And I helped her and Sky get closer, Lisha added in her mind. *I only hope that it's temporary.*

"Hey, I hope you guys still plan to give me that party," Karma said, reaching into the drawer for a sharp knife to cut the bagels. "I want a blowout."

"We do," Chelsea promised. "How's next weekend?"

"I want to invite the cute doctor from the hospital," Karma said, digging into the ice cream again.

"Demetrius isn't enough for you?" Lisha teased.

"This guy isn't for me," Karma said. "But you can never have too many fine guys at a party. Besides, he's too nice not to invite."

"You mean too cute," Chelsea teased.

"Well, yeah," Karma agreed. "I swear, he's got dimples. And really broad shoulders—"

"And a killer bedside manner," Lisha added, taking the sharp knife from Karma.

She began to cut the bagels in half. For the first time since she'd received the phone call from Dr. de Souza, she felt hopeful.

Maybe I really will get good news tomorrow, she thought. *I'm not coughing anymore. Maybe I'll get my life back. And Sky. And a future—*

"Lisha!" Chelsea yelped.

Lisha stood there, dumbfounded. While daydreaming, she had managed to slice right through both the bagel and her finger. Blood dripped onto the counter.

Poison blood.

Deadly blood.

"Get back, both of you!" Lisha yelled.

Karma and Chelsea just stood there, paralyzed.

"Just . . . get out of the kitchen!"

Chelsea fought back her panic. "It's okay, Lish. Just clean it up. It's not important."

"Yes, it is! My blood could kill you!"

"Lish—" Karma began.

"Please, just . . . just get out of the kitchen! I mean it. Please."

Silently, Chelsea and Karma went into the living room. As tears poured down Lisha's face she tore off some paper towels and mopped up her blood. She wrapped a towel around her bleeding finger. She ran a sponge under the hot water until it was scalding hot, and then she rubbed viciously at the spot on the counter where she had bled. Long after the blood was cleaned up, she continued to rub at the spot.

"Lisha, it's okay," Chelsea said quietly, coming up behind her.

"It's not okay," Lisha said, pausing for a moment. She went into her bathroom and got a box of Band-Aids. She wrapped four of them around the small cut. Then she went back into the kitchen and attacked the counter with the sponge and hot water again.

"Come on," Chelsea said. "Really."

She took Lisha's hand and led her into the living room. Lisha sat heavily on the couch. She buried her head in her hands. "Oh, God. I'm so scared. . . ."

Chelsea and Karma came and sat on either side of Lisha. They both put their arms around her, and they let her cry.

12

"**D**o you want coffee?" Chelsea asked Lisha as they stood in the kitchen together the next morning.

Lisha shook her head no. She hadn't slept at all. There were huge, dark circles under her eyes. She filled a glass of water at the sink. Her hands were trembling.

Karma came in and poured herself a cup of coffee. No one said anything.

"What time is it?" Lisha finally asked. Her watch had stopped working the day before.

"Almost nine," Karma replied. "Are you hungry?" she asked Lisha.

"I may never eat again," Lisha managed.

There was a knock on the front door. Chelsea hurried to open it. It was Alan.

"Hey, Karma!" he said happily when he saw her. He gave her a big hug. "I didn't know you were here."

"I'm visiting," Karma said. "But soon I'll be back for good."

"We all miss you," Alan told her. He turned to Lisha. "It's really beautiful out. I already spent two hours down by the river writing. You want to do brunch?"

No one said a word. Alan looked around at the pinched, anxious faces of his friends. "Did someone die?"

Me, maybe, Lisha thought. "No. We're just . . . busy," she told him.

Alan came over to her and peered at her. "Lish? I thought you were over your bronchitis."

"I am," she said.

"But you look terrible." Alan's voice was filled with concern. He felt her forehead. "No fever. In fact, you feel cold."

"I'm okay," she insisted.

"Good," he replied, though he didn't look convinced. "Sky told me that you and he . . . that you're not together," he added, his voice low.

"Uh, Karma and I will go . . . do something or other in my room," Chelsea said, dragging Karma down the hall so Lisha and Alan could talk.

"That's true," Lisha agreed.

Alan nodded. "I'd be lying if I said I wasn't happy about it."

"I can't talk about this now, Alan," Lisha said. "I'm sorry."

His eyes searched hers. "No matter what

happens, Lisha, I'm your friend. You know that, don't you?"

Lisha nodded.

Alan smiled his lopsided grin. "I seem to make a better friend than I do a boyfriend, huh?" he asked wistfully.

"I'll take all the friends I can get, Alan," Lisha said.

His hand gently wrapped around her wrist. "You've lost weight, Lish. Look how little you are!" He held up her wrist.

"And just think, this time I lost weight without becoming a drug addict," she said bitterly.

Yeah. I'm dying, instead, she added in her mind.

No. You can't think that way, she ordered herself, as if her thought processes were somehow going to affect the outcome of her HIV test.

"You worry about your weight too much," Alan said. "Didn't anyone ever tell you that beauty comes from within?"

"Yeah," Lisha said, smiling at him in spite of her fears, "but you're the only guy I know who really believes it."

" 'She walks in beauty, like the night,' " Alan quoted. "That's how I think of you."

"I don't feel very beautiful."

Alan sat with Lisha on the couch. "That reminds me of my mom. She was so beautiful when I was a kid. But my father was so hard on her—always making her feel insecure, you know—she wasn't ever thin enough or perfect enough for him. So she never got to enjoy her own beauty. Like you."

"You're such a poet," Lisha told him.

"Nah, I write terrible poetry," Alan said. "I'm hoping that I don't write terrible novels. I . . . I might have a first draft done soon."

"Really? That's so wonderful!"

"Maybe not," Alan said. "Maybe everything I wrote is awful."

"I'm sure that's not true," Lisha protested.

"Would you . . . would you read it? When I'm done, I mean?"

"I'd love to," Lisha told him.

He leaned over and kissed her cheek. "You sure I can't take you to brunch?"

Lisha shook her head no. "I have . . . an appointment."

Alan got up and gently pulled her to her feet. "Okay, then. But I'm coming over later to make sure you're all right."

She walked him to the door. After she let him out, she closed her eyes and leaned against the frame. *Please, God,* she prayed. *Let me be all right. Let me live.*

She had no idea if God answered prayers like that. Or not. But it seemed to her that too many horrible things happened in the world to too many innocent, religious people to believe that God would do something about her prayer.

Which meant she was on her own.

"Alan left?" Chelsea asked as she and Karma came back into the living room.

"Yeah," Lisha said. "Is it time to go?"

Chelsea nodded.

"Well, let's go, then," Lisha said. She picked up her small pack and slung the slender strap over her shoulder.

Wordlessly, the three of them left the apartment.

"How can she keep us waiting for so long?" Lisha was pacing back and forth in the cramped waiting room outside Dr. de Souza's office at the health department.

"She'll be out soon," Chelsea assured her.

"Or maybe I'm better off waiting forever," Lisha said, pacing again. "Maybe I don't want to know."

A skinny guy with bad skin sitting next to Karma looked up at her.

He probably has AIDS, too, Lisha thought. *He's probably just like me.*

Her hollow stomach turned over with fear.

"Mark Grayton?" a nurse asked, entering the waiting room. The skinny guy rose from his chair and followed her down the hall.

"I saw a coffee machine outside," Karma said. "I could—"

"I don't want any," Lisha said. She paced again. "I hate this."

"Lisha?"

She looked up.

It was Sky. He looked nervous, but so beautiful. He had on a blue T-shirt and faded jeans. To Lisha, he looked perfect.

"What are you doing here?" she asked, walking over to him. He opened his mouth. "No, wait," she interrupted. "Don't tell me. My bigmouthed roommate told you." She glared at Chelsea.

"I didn't tell him anything," Chelsea insisted, putting down the magazine she had been pretending to read.

"Me, either," Karma said.

"No one told me anything," Sky said. "I . . . I followed you from our apartment. I've been pacing outside for the past half hour, trying to get up the nerve to come in here."

"You *followed* me?" Lisha echoed incredulously. "That's . . . that's sick!"

"Look, I'm sorry," Sky said, "but I know something is going on that you're not telling me about. I just had to find out—"

"I can't believe you followed me."

"Believe it," Sky said.

"I don't owe you any explanations for anything," Lisha said, her voice cold.

"No, you don't," Sky agreed. "But I thought you might actually care about me enough to let me share what's going on with you."

"I . . . I don't," Lisha managed. "So please, just go away."

"Lish—" Chelsea protested.

"Don't you dare say a word." Lisha warned her friend. "I want Sky to leave."

"I'm not leaving!" Sky announced. He reached for Lisha's arm. "I know what goes on here, Lisha. A friend of mine got tested for hepatitis here last year. You think you're sick, don't you?"

Lisha didn't answer.

"Do you have hepatitis? Is that what's going on? Did you really think I'd care if you have hepatitis?"

"I don't have . . . hepatitis," Lisha said carefully.

"Herpes, then?" Sky asked. "Look, there's nothing that's so terrible that we can't deal with it, can't you see that?"

"Just go away, Sky."

"No," he said. "I'm not leaving you. I know you don't really want me to—"

"Yes, I do!"

Tears glistened in Sky's eyes. "I'm not going to let you push me away, Lisha."

"You have to," she cried.

"Why?" he asked, his voice rising with frustration. "Just tell me why!"

"Because I have AIDS!"

Sky's face turned white. He was speechless.

"That changes everything, doesn't it?" Lisha asked bitterly.

"She doesn't know if she's HIV positive," Chelsea explained. "She had a blood test. We're waiting for the results."

"Harley was a drug addict," Lisha said. "He died HIV positive and he didn't even know it. This other girl he was sleeping with in Europe, behind my back, is HIV positive, and she got it from him. And I'm next."

"You . . . you don't know that," Sky whispered.

"Yeah," Lisha said. "I do."

"You don't," Karma interjected. "So don't keep saying you do."

"The words don't mean anything," Lisha said, still staring at Sky. "The facts are the facts. And any minute now that nurse is going to call my name. And I'm going to sit in that doctor's office. And she's going to read me my death sentence." Tears filled her eyes. "So don't tell me that nothing is so terrible that we can't get through it together, Sky. Because it's a big, fat lie."

Sky reached out and touched her hair.

"Don't," Lisha said, stepping away from him.

"I'm not afraid," he told her, his voice low.

"You should be," Lisha said, her lips trembling.

"Lisha." Sky opened his arms. He put them around Lisha.

Just this once, she told herself. *Just let me have his arms around me one last time.*

She moved into the circle of Sky's embrace. His arms closed around her. And for a moment she could pretend that everything was normal.

"I'm not leaving you, Lisha," he whispered into her hair.

"Lisha Bishop?" the nurse called.

Oh, God.

Lisha stepped out of Sky's arms. "Yes," she said, forcing herself to remain steady. "I'm ready."

Chelsea and Karma got up quickly.

"Just Miss Bishop," the nurse said.

"I don't think so," Karma said. "We're coming, too."

"That's not the way we do it," the nurse said huffily.

"Yeah, well, that's the way we do it," Lisha said, holding her head high.

Sky came to her and took her hand. Karma and Chelsea stood on her other side.

The nurse shrugged. "Dr. de Souza can handle it, I'm out of it." She turned. They followed her down the hall.

Dr. de Souza's office was as cramped as Lisha remembered it. She sat. A fly landed on the doctor's framed diploma from Rutgers University medical school on the wall.

Sky stood behind her, his hands on her neck.

The room was silent. The seconds felt like hours, ticking by. Lisha could hear the pounding of her own heart.

Finally, Dr. de Souza came into the office. "Hello again, Lisha," she said kindly. She shut the door after her. Then she sat behind her desk and opened a file.

Please. God. Please. Don't let it be positive.

"I have the results of your HIV test," Dr. de Souza said, her eyes not meeting Lisha's.

"Yes," Lisha said.

"This test is not one hundred percent accurate," the doctor said. "It's important that you know that. There is an additional, more accurate test we can do."

Sky's hands tightened on Lisha's shoulders.

Dr. de Souza smoothed some of her flyaway hair into her messy bun. Finally she looked up at Lisha.

Please. I'll do anything, God, Lisha prayed. *I'll be a better person. Just please, don't let my test be positive. Let me live. Please. I want to live.*

The doctor cleared her throat.

And before she spoke, Lisha knew.

"I'm sorry, Lisha," the doctor said. "But your HIV test was positive."

THE TRASH CAN

Hey, Cherie!
Subj: The TRASHiest series ever!
From: CuteGurl6@aol.com
To: authorchik@aol.com

Hi! My name is Missy and I think *Trash* is my absolute favorite book series! I just got done reading *Good Girls, Bad Boys.* My favorite book so far is #1, *Trash.* I think *Trash* would make a good TV show. I mean it's just a soap opera, but a book. And I absolutely love it. I'm only twelve but I already love it! (I'm mature for my age, if you think twelve is too young—I got all As on my last report card, with the exception of one B in PE.) Well I also like your Sunset books. I just got done reading *Sunset Fling*, and I plan on reading others.

One of your many fans,
Missy

Hey, Missy!
Yours is one of many, many letters that have come in by e-mail about *Trash.* As you know, there's a whole online community of your sister readers out there on the Internet. Anyone who'd like to join in on the fun just needs to send me an e-mail at authorchik@aol.com, and I'll send you the online newsletter, keypal info, Web site addresses (or just search YAHOO! under "Cherie Bennett"), a booklist, etc.

Cherie

Hey, Cherie and Jeff!

I think the *Trash* series is so cool. I just finished *Good Girls, Bad Boys.* It was so great, I could never put it down. I finally have read a book that seems realistic to me. I could never relate to having a mass murderer as a father, a crazy ex from London, or being adopted by Jewish hippies, but that could happen in real life, and that's what's cool about *Trash*! How about a book from a guy's point of view?

Thanks,
Ashley Green

Hey, Ashley!

I could never relate to having a mass murderer for a father, either, although my father did have a local TV show in Detroit when I was growing up called *Meet Mr. Satan,* where he showed late night horror movies and dressed up like a ghoul and lived in a coffin. He kept the coffin in our basement, and kids used to come over to see it. Can you imagine? As for books from a guy's point of view, you should really have enjoyed this one, and I'd like to do even more on that idea in future books. Keep reading!

Cherie

Write to us or e-mail us, okay? We wanna hear from you!

snail mail: Cherie & Jeff
P.O. Box 150326
Nashville, TN 37215
e-mail: authorchik@aol.com